lay with me, lie with me

elizabeth coffee

My fervid thanks to everyone who encouraged and supported me, those of you who read and re-read, made suggestions, made corrections, made me struggle on.

Special thanks to Ida Rae Egli who tolerated my obsessive compulsions throughout; to Wendy Platt who cried with me when I wiped the whole novel off my computer; to Emily and John Vedouras who translated my poems into Greek; to Russell Hardy, who found Emily and John Vedouras; and to my husband and best friend, Jim, who never lost faith.

Platt & Company

ISBN 0-9765581-0-6
copyright 2005

JUSTINA

Each single one of our citizens, in all
the manifold aspects of life, is able to
show himself the rightful lord and
owner of his own person, and do this,
moreover, with exceptional versatility.
Pericles (c. 495-429 B.C.)
Athens, Greece

CHAPTER ONE

The white Datsun truck cut in front of them dangerously on the slick road.

Wil jammed on the brakes and swore under his breath to avoid a collision. Justina smiled in spite of herself—the ubiquitous white Datsun. This one even had a black tool box slung across the shoulders of the bed like Sasha's. But she knew it wasn't Sasha's when she saw the Jesus bumper sticker in iridescent script letters on the left side of the tailgate, and on the other side: Will you go to Heaven or Hell?

"Oh, Hell, for sure," she thought, but continued to smile. "At least if society and the clergy are right.

"On the other hand, if I am right, I've experienced a kind of heaven already, and it might be that we can't have heaven on earth and in the afterlife, too. And since I'm not too sure about the afterlife, I'll take what I've had…"

Wil glanced across at her, surprised to see the smirky smile and expression of contentment after their near miss. He laid his hand on her knee. "Excited?"

"Um, yes, of course."

They were on their way to the airport in an unusual downpour for this desert city, and driving was bad enough in clement weather; in the rain, few knew enough to reduce their speed, or if they knew, cared to moderate their speed and be cautious.

Justina continued to ruminate, the white Datsun truck reminding her of Sasha, the lover she was leaving behind. Next to her, Wil, her husband, who had become… "What?" she thought. "…good friend, companion, loyal, father of their grown children, but no longer lover. She allowed herself to sorrow silently. Where did all that early passion go? Does it have to get lost somewhere between the snotty noses, sore throats, and the angst of teenagers, college funds and the empty nest or did they just let it go? Does it die a natural death or does the disease of apathy and time slowly take its toll—an unknown, but still cancerous tumor eating away at the life of love?

"But the host survives," she thought, "and hope along with it—my own eagerness for experience and passion and freedom from what has become this hypocrisy—a warm, nurturing, pleasant hypocrisy, but hypocrisy, nonetheless."

She sighed softly and thought again of Sasha.

The truck ahead of them sped through a large puddle and sent an elegant spray into the air which fell in arcs to earth. Just like her love for Sasha, it had the same qualities of fireworks and elusiveness. She held the image captive—the sparks rising and gracefully creating the outburst—but the reality had already dissipated.

How many times during the past year had she been on this same freeway, dashing to one appointment or another, rushing to make a class on time, when she would look up and there it was—a white Datsun truck—never Sasha's. But whatever she had been thinking, this new image exploded in her head, unbidden. "Sasha." She wondered just how many white trucks Datsun produced and whether they had sold all of them here, so often had it happened.

She assured her herself now that when she got to New York, she would be free of this vision. Surely it would be yellow cabs and black limousines.

The truck moved into the center lane, and as they passed, she had a brief glance of a red plastic rose swinging from the rear view mirror. "Of course. What else would it be?" she thought.

Because it had all begun with three red roses. And she rejected it, even as she thought it, an asinine statement because, of course, nothing starts at a beginning one can later identify. One can't say, "Yes, it all began here, at this particular juncture." An affair is a dance that begins long before the orchestra sounds the first note. The side-long glances—"Will you say yes if I ask you to dance?"—are already too late, not the start. And first love is the dance of all dances, the opening night at a performance when two stars collide with an atomic blast on an atoll of barren landscapes—and the partners want to remain in that non-toxic mushroom cloud lost over the vast sea, isolated and alone together. First love shapes the dancers and the dance forever; something they know and want to remember, but then later forget—or ignore. New music and rhythms assault their ears, play different tunes and it is never the same again.

Every later love affair or lustful liaison dares the dancers to step on the toes of first love as they struggle to recapture or escape its power over them. But they deliberately re-choreograph new steps and gestures, carefully avoiding a misstep.

So how was it even possible for Justina to know where and how it all started? Her life was smooth, uneventful and unexciting for the most part, and she was comfortable; certainly not searching for the chaos that was about to descend upon her. Butterfly wings gently swooped over a flower continents away, and she was unaware that change with a capital "C" had already begun the slow but dramatic erosion of her life as she knew it.

Her myopic brown eyes rested on him briefly along with the others as she introduced herself to the class she was teaching to mostly blue collar workers at a large manufacturing plant. She had limited knowledge of what was made there. It didn't really matter—some kind of widgets, she suspected, for the Government, since she needed a badge and an escort to the training room. She was asked to do this class as a favor because the professor of the prior class had "created problems."

Added to the dissatisfaction of the students with the prof was another issue: unfiled, but charges nevertheless, that a student had cheated in some way on a paper he was required to write. Every professor who went there after that was notified "to monitor him carefully." Justina hated that aspect of university life—the gossip about students who were unable to defend themselves simply because no one had the guts to go public with their accusations but defamed the students in the halls of academe anyway.

And then, of course, there's the paperwork and attendance

rosters so students' loans (and the university's financials) could be monitored and both found to be compliant. So it was, while taking attendance, that Justina got a lesson in how to roll her tongue around the name, Alexander Psipsopoulos. It wasn't only the tongue rolling but getting the accent just right. And then after all that to learn he was called Sasha, the diminutive of Alexander in Croatia, but not in Greece; his mother a Croat, his father Greek.

Of course he and his peers loved it—here she was in her power suit looking for all the world like "Bloomies" second floor, but she was on the second floor of this monstrous, noisy factory: the smell of grease and grime and chemicals flirting with her nostrils, cables snaking everywhere, 24-hours-a-day of whirring and pounding, of behemoth, complicated looking—and, indeed, they had to be complicated—engines and machines three stories high with conveyor belts, chains, blocks and tackles, items she could not name. And this was their territory!

Justina learned a lot from Sasha about the ability of her tongue to roll around objects, but she never quite mastered the accent on his surname. Did she care? Not at all. Given the two skills, she much preferred the lessons on the former to the latter.

Sasha was no ordinary young man. In the Southwestern United States his Eastern European/Mediterranean accent made him different. Hispanic and the song of Mexico was familiar. Croatian laced with Greek? Decidedly unusual and exotic. But it was more than that; Justina grew to appreciate the elegance of his English and his particular (sometimes peculiar) use of the language. In the way of many for whom English is a second language, he spoke more slowly, thoughtfully, sometimes still searching for exactly the right word. But his choice of words was learned and proper, intelligent (and could be bawdy and suggestive, for he had learned the standard slang as well).

He also looked unusual and exotic in a dark, brooding, Heathcliff kind of way, and Justina caught glimpses of a kind of moroseness amid the ready laughter and charm he exuded among his classmates. But it was his eyes that were orbs of delight—seeing, she knew immediately, beyond the surface and probing for the essence of everything! His was the best mind in the room although others were certainly higher placed on the organizational chart. It's rare to find the kind of creativity or originality of thought that Sasha exhibited—to go beyond the case study, to do the extra reading, to take the material and experiment with it and then analyze the results.

So he was the Everystudent every teacher yearns for: intelligent, curious, slightly cocky, even arrogant, but one who instinctively knew his limits. Did she ever during that semester entertain lewd and lascivious thoughts about him? She would have been appalled if such had been suggested. "My God, you're talking about the stuff the tabloids dream about—I'm old enough to be his mother."

He told Justina later that members of his study group frequently said, "She likes you, Sasha." And Justina responded, "Of course I liked you." They were in bed, and he moved his body closer to press up against her, "What was there not to like? But this? Not then..."

And it wasn't only Justina who appreciated his quick wit and intelligence. Sasha had come to the university to register for a new class when Justina and a colleague passed him in a hallway with the requisite "Hi-how-are-you's." Her companion turned to Justina and said, "There's a great student. I really like him." And Justina thought, "Not as much as I do." But that was much later.

She was challenged by this class and when it ended, Justina realized she had a new appreciation for what she was doing. She tried explaining it to Wil while she was filling out the grade sheet. "You know," she mused, "Somehow this class has changed me. I remember my father taking night classes after work when I was a kid, and I see that desire to do better, become something more in these students who are working in a factory."

She turned philosophical. "Isn't that exactly what the American dream is all about? Not to be stuck where you are, but to move to where you want to be? I loved every minute of it. I loved the factory. Who invents those machines any way and how? The thousands of pieces that go into them with the pulleys and cams and moving parts all designed to do something specific. It's absolutely amazing. I could watch the flow forever and contemplate the minds that created them—and then, at the end something new and entirely different—but even that is only a part of some other whole."

Wil didn't respond, and she continued on, dreamily...

"I feel as if I've hatched from a cocoon—not too much removed from this group—as if we are all caught in the chrysalis of possibility and struggling to escape, but attached to the sticky threads of the past and the accident of our births."

But Wil was poring over a new contract, so he only looked up and smiled indulgently before he resumed his work.

And Justina, instead of contemplating the minds that had created those fascinating machines, contemplated Wagner's "Siegfried Idyll" and knew, therefore, that all things were possible; improbable, most of them, but possible. And she was seduced by the possibility...

CHAPTER TWO

Justina glanced at her watch as she hurried down the hall to meet with her students individually. Ten minutes. And she still had to use the bathroom. Several of them were gathered in a cluster around the door, so she knew it was locked. Damn! There goes the bathroom. Why can't Security be more efficient? Now to go find someone herself or send one of the students.

"Okay. Who's got the five o'clock?"

Carol said, "I do, and I need to be out of here in twenty minutes."

"Well, who's got the five thirty?"

The pipefitter raised his hand.

"Well, can I ask you to find Security? Then Carol and I can begin out here."

"Sure." And he ambled off.

"Okay, Carol. How's it going?"

These were to be one-on-one sessions with the students she hadn't seen for almost a year. During that time, they were supposed to have done their literature review for the research projects they were attempting and come to this meeting with the bare bones of their surveys.

Carol looked down, and Justina knew from that glance to prepare herself for the inevitable excuses: My mother was ill and I had just enough time to keep up with my other classes. My teenager was arrested for drug abuse and is in a rehab program. I had to travel for my job. My husband left—never did like the fact that I was going to college. And so it went. She had heard variations of these themes before. In the beginning, she was sympathetic and she hurt for them. After all, she, above all, knew how difficult it was to juggle family, job, school even when everything went smoothly. But she grew to realize that no life is smooth, even when it seems to be, and for some, mere blips on the road of life turned into detours with barricades that also provided excuses. So she could empathize and sympathize, but somewhere deep inside her, she felt more and more inured to it all.

"I tried, Justina, I really did, but my son was caught with drugs, the hard stuff, so juvenile court and all that stuff, and now he's at Westwood in rehab, and we're in family counseling—twice a week. Classes, once a week; study group—well they've been carrying me, so…" Her voice trailed off.

They were still standing in the hall, and other students were approaching.

"All right, Carol. Where are you and what's your plan?"

Justina ignored the tears she could see wanting to escape, held in check, but only barely so, and she put her hand on Carol's shoulder. "Look, let's see what you've got and whether we can salvage it somehow."

Carol visibly relaxed, and the pipefitter, "Damn, what is his name?" Justina thought, came strolling up, triumphant, the blue-shirted uniformed Security in tow. "Well, at least I know his name." she thought. "Thank you, Richard," she smiled after a glance at his left pocket.

"No problem," he smiled in return. "See ya' at ten."

They took seats at one of the long tables as the small group of students whose time had not yet come, clustered at a far away table talking in low, respectful tones.

"Without your literature review, Carol, you're out there. If you don't know what's already been done and discovered, you don't have a basis for your own research. Do you have a list of sources?" A shamed nod from Carol. "Can you squeeze one more hour out of your day for awhile? How about your lunch hour?"

Another silent nod. "But we only have thirty minutes for lunch…"

"Right. But that's still good—maybe that's better—a half hour at lunch and another half hour sometime before you go to bed or get up early? I've found smaller pieces of information and ideas sometimes come together better than spending hours at a task when you get kind of loco keeping them all straight. You know, many great thinkers slept on the ideas that came to them during the day and had dreams and epiphanies when they were involved in other things that led them forward. Maybe that will happen to you. So do you think you can begin there? Is that do-able?"

Another nod, this time more enthusiastic. "All right. Look, you had a half hour appointment with me. Do you have any of your stuff with you?"

"Yeah, I guess I brought it so I could convince you I was trying."

"I never doubted you were trying… Okay. We've spent ten minutes together on a half-hour interview. So you have twenty minutes to spare. Go over to that table in the corner and try to sort out what you have. Make a plan; oh, damn, you said you had to be out of here in twenty minutes. Carol, start to work even for the next ten minutes to break this up into smaller pieces—plan how you're going to do this. I know you can. Try not to keep looking at the big picture. Once you have the smaller pieces, you'll be able to accomplish them one at a time. If you fail for a thirty-minute increment, it's not the same as total failure. You'll be able to make up that thirty minutes somewhere else along the way. Keep it small and underwhelming, you know?"

Justina leaned over the papers neither of them had examined and put her arm around Carol's shoulder. "You can do it; I know you can. You have my telephone number and my e-mail. Call for help—or support—or questions—whatever—when you need to. You know what you have to do?"

Carol nodded affirmatively, and then the tears, embarrassing them both fell silently, tears of gratitude and relief, tears of exhaustion and hope. "Thank you…"

"Just go do it. I know you can." And Justina, for all her cynicism about excuses felt she really needed to go cry somewhere as well.

Fragile souls, how to make them stronger? And immediately, she realized she had what? eight minutes left before the next interview and she could go to the bathroom.

She excused herself from the next student who was already approaching, pointedly glancing at her watch. "Back in a minute."

And so it was she encountered Sasha in the hall, leaning against the wall. "You're the last one on my list," she said.

"I know. No problem. I'll wait."

And with her unsettled emotions, she went into the lavatory, relieved herself and briefly shed her own tears for Carol and all the Carols (and the Georges) in her classes.

Sasha was nowhere in sight when she emerged, but she saw Carol at the end of the hall leaving with someone. Sasha? She couldn't see...

Multiple interviews—some mirroring the one she had had with Carol except like fun-house mirrors: each had a twist of its own blurring the reality and the pain; huge things diminished to a pimple and small things blown up to tornado-like proportions with similar devastation; surreal and poignant images of the facts—and some straight forward; the students prepared. It was nine-thirty, and Sasha appeared.

"Carol and I found out it was your birthday today, so..." And from behind his back, he produced three red roses and shyly handed them across the table. Briefly, Justina remembered Sasha had said, almost under his breath as they were leaving their last class, "If you were not my professor, I would tell you some things about how I feel about you" in his sometimes fractured English, and Justina thought at the time it was appreciation for her efforts in class. She acknowledged his comment then with a smile. If she had thought about it at all, it was with the knowledge that even older students, like first graders, sometimes develop crushes on their teachers.

The roses were in one of those glass bud vases that florists must buy by the thousands, the buds themselves still in individual woven plastic thread girdles. She had never seen flowers so constrained. Later she realized that the little webbed cages contained the buds so that they would remain erect, but she also had a fleeting moment when it pained her to see them so—so many cages in the world with so many worthwhile reasons for making sure things seem to be not as they are or would become, but as we want to see them—under control. There was a florist's card woven, too, between the tines of a plastic fork, and written on it, "Thank you. Carol and Sasha."

"Thank you. Thank you both. I'm starting to try not remembering my birthday, but this is very nice. I won't ask how you found out it was my birthday." Justina smiled, and began moving papers around in front of her somewhat nervously. She moved the roses off to the side. "Okay, let's see what you have."

Sasha was one of the ones who was prepared. He was working on a time-and-motion study using Frederick W. Taylor's work, and he had devised charts for observation of each production task he was studying, as well as individual time sheets for each worker. "I've decided to assign costs to each task as well and include a cost-benefits analysis. Waddya' think?" he asked.

"I think you're expanding this beyond your original questions and your hypothesis, and that's great if you'll be able to complete it in the time you have left. How much more work will it entail?"

And much before they were finished discussing the details of this addition to his project, Richard, the security guard, appeared. He was pointed in letting them know it was time to go, pulling his arm out of his sleeve to glance at his watch. He needed to lock up.

They began gathering up papers, still talking about his project. "Look, if I buy you a drink, could I buy a little more of your time? I still have some questions, and it is your birthday…"

She considered briefly. It wasn't at all unusual to meet with students over a cup of coffee or even lunch, and she wondered why she even hesitated. Then, "Sure. Where shall we go?"

"There's a Mexican restaurant out on the highway—the Coq d'Or—you know it?"

"Yes, I think so. On the corner?"

"Yeah. I'll meet you there, okay?"

Justina had second thoughts as she got into her car. But why? She dismissed them. What was the big deal?

After ordering her glass of wine and his beer, they began where they had left off. He continued to rationalize the benefits of the costs involved. "After all," he said, "what they're really interested in is the bottom line. This way I can verify not only the efficiency, but also how the costs are accrued and whether we can save money and how much. Remember, you're the one who told us it was not only the five W's but the two H's—your own variation on those rules: Who, What, Where, When, Why and How, and you added How Much. So I decided to see how much."

She laughed. "I guess you've got me. I'm just concerned that you don't get in over your head on this thing. Remember you have to be concerned about deadlines." He nodded in agreement. "So fix the first chapter to include the cost-benefits analysis, and make sure you expand your literature search. I have the feeling that since you've made this decision, I won't be able to talk you out of it."

And they began to talk about the university, other classes, touched briefly on Carol's troubles, and their drinks were consumed.

They left and he walked her to her car. Impulsively, as she turned from unlocking the car door to say good night, he hugged her, "Thank you. Thank you for everything. And happy birthday."

CHAPTER THREE

Later, she couldn't remember how she got the roses home, but she did remember that on her desk were a dozen roses from Wil, sent that morning of her birthday.

When they were all well past their prime and she was readying them for the trash, she removed the card signed by Sasha and Carol, and was about to throw it into the waste basket under her desk when she saw some writing on the reverse side—several lines hand written in what she thought at the time was Cyrillic; it did not look like Greek to her, although it was certainly Greek to her. And it had the appearance of a poem: four lines. And until she knew what was written, she left the three roses and tucked the card into her wallet.

Τό χαμόγελο στό πρόσωπό σου... Ω! τό πρόσωπό σου...

Χαμένο από τη θέα μου

Γίνεται ένα δάκρυ

Όταν δέν είμαι μαζί σου.

The next night was the last meeting of the entire class. She would not see any of them again until graduation. Their projects would go to the university committee in another three months for final approval, and the rest was up to them.

Justina announced she had something she needed translated from Cyrillic, or Greek, she wasn't sure. All heads turned to Sasha, and he, eyebrows raised, shrugged. Said he'd try.

"Later," she said, "if there is time after class."

But they had used up the few minutes after class was over before it was time to lock up, and they were still discussing strategy for his project. So here they were at the Coq d'Or again—at Sasha's suggestion.

With apologies for his inability to accurately translate from Greek to English, he told her the essence of the poem, one he had written as a youth. "I never showed it to anyone before…"

The smile on your face — oh, your face —
Missing from my view
Becomes a tear
When I am not with you…

The thought of the first grader with a crush on his teacher flashed across her thoughts. That she could deal with, but this was no first grader. This was a very attractive man and she was a woman. Warning bells were going off at regular intervals, but she ignored them, choosing to concentrate on his project.

His manager was balking at the idea of this low-level person upstaging him in his own department. They went through all the steps and phases: His manager had already approved the project—they both had signed copies of his approval; indeed, the approval had already been sent to the university. He had been granted access to the people on the line. "I don't think he's going to say 'No' to my face, but he's going to, how-do-you-say, put abstracts in the way."

"You mean 'obstacles'?" she asked.

"Yes. What did I say?"

"Abstracts—well, obstacles might very well be abstract, but they'll still be there, won't they?"

"Yeah—yes." He was discouraged, but also bitter. "I don't understand, Tina, how everyone is always saying, 'Cut costs. More production. Less time.' and now that I want to quantify it to see how and if it can be done, this cretin isn't going to help me."

"Cretin. That's a good word for many managers…"

"I remember it because it's close to Croatian—and God knows I left Croatia to do better things—like this—in the USA, and then instead I find your country populated with these cretins. You know, you're all pretty strange in this country, not like I imagined." And then, quickly, before she could reply, "Forget that. You are not strange, but in this country people do some really weird things." And then, feeling safer with another subject, "Like burning your flag."

"Burning our flag?"

"Yes, that makes me very angry when I read about it in the paper and see it on TV. I don't understand why you allow it to happen. I don't mean you, you know what I mean. Those people should be in jail."

"But it's considered a form of free speech."

"Bah. Sometimes people shouldn't say everything that comes into their mind." And as if that idea, too, should not be pursued, he became quiet.

They were turned sideways, sitting on the banquette, her knees tucked up, casual, and were silent.

"Okay, let's talk about other things." And he motioned the waiter and without asking, ordered two more drinks.

The late evening became even later as they talked "about other things." His arm lay across the banquette, and occasionally, his hand dropped to her shoulder to make a point. She did not withdraw nor pretend to be offended.

Perhaps it was that second drink (his or hers?), but that hand also lay on her knee as the conversation became more personal and intense.

It was no single one word, not a single idea or topic, but somehow the air in that restaurant changed. The smell of the corn tortillas being warmed in the oven, the sweetness of the onions, the spices which had greeted them when they pushed open the door gave way to the scent of just the two of them, sitting close enough so that they were both aware of it. Someone looking at them from across the room would have imagined them to be lovers, intense and concentrated only on each other, oblivious to their surroundings. Justina heard those earlier warning bells, but their sound had turned lyrical and melodious.

She was sure she had not in some way given Sasha tacit permission to touch her, but she also did not withdraw. Why? She asked herself that very same question a million times over. Even as they sat there with his hand moving along her thigh, in some other sane part of her mind, she kept asking, "What are you doing?" But it was a question she was asking herself, not Sasha. She knew what he was doing, and she liked it.

When they got to her car, Sasha didn't wait alongside her but walked casually around to the passenger side and opened the car door when it was unlocked. They got into the car wordlessly, she looking straight ahead, he turned sideways to look at her, both waiting for the other to say the first word, make the first move. He, to be asked to leave; she not wanting to do that.

"This is crazy," she finally whispered, still staring out the windshield.

"Why?" he asked.

"For many reasons."

"Say," in a quiet voice.

She turned to him now. Hard as it was, she squeezed the words out. "Well, for one thing we are both married. Then there is that other thing—the matter of our ages…"

Ignoring the issue of their marriages, he uttered, "I knew you would say that. Why does that matter?"

"Everything—all of it matters—it matters all over the place. I would look absolutely ridiculous if anyone knew I was here with you contemplating what we're contemplating—the age certainly, but there are the ethics of our professor/student relationship for another. Wait, I'll think of more…"

"I am not your student any more. That ended tonight, remember? Class is over, teacher," gently teasing. "I will fix the project; the committee will praise it and me, and incidentally, you…"

He leaned over, and kissed her gently but insistently. Now she knew she had somehow given him permission to do this—that somehow he was touching her naked body even though she was fully clothed. Had he mentally undressed her in class? She smiled, wanly. He pulled back. "What?"

"I just can't get beyond how crazy this is." Another car pulled into the parking lot.

"See? See? It's the police. Can't you just see the headlines in the morning paper? 'University professor, chair of her department, arrested for molesting younger student in car outside local restaurant.' My colleagues will never stop laughing. I'll be brought up on ethics charges. My mailbox on campus (assuming I still have a job) will be full before I get there. There'll be confirmations for hotel reservations all over the city, bogus checks made out to hotels with my signature, all sorts of things—condoms, leaflets on safe sex. Faculty have a cruel sense of humor about this kind of thing. And with good reason. We're supposed to be above seduction."

"You can stay on the bottom if that's what you wish…" and he grinned wickedly, shyly.

They were soon all but undressed. "Slip off your panties, Tina." And then they were both undressed from the waist down, doing all those wonderful things people do to each other in the front seat of cars. Front seats are not quite so forgiving as back seats, and little European sports cars are the least forgiving of all. They may look sexy, but they turn the sex act into a gymnastic feat.

Still, Justina knew she had let herself be seduced by this young man, and in spite of the very real problems she knew she now faced, she had savored every delicious moment of it. She shivered with pleasure as her body remembered his hands gently caressing places she didn't even know belonged to her. She could taste the remnants of that last beer he had drunk, bitter and acid in the glass made sweet with his saliva, the heat of his mouth. His gasps of pleasure mingled with her own cries pounded in her head till she thought her ears would send out sound waves of their own but it was a mute thunder that she felt rather than heard.

CHAPTER FOUR

S he was reading the paper in bed the next morning, his now dead roses on her breakfast tray, but she didn't care. She was glad, so glad, she hadn't thrown them out. She had something he had touched. Better, it was a gift—well, half a gift from him, some evidence that he existed. He was real. The roses were evidence. There was a card with his name on it, his poem. TO HER! Glory, glory, why her? Did she need to know? Probably, but not right now. For now she was content to be fifteen again, instead of fifty-one.

When she had prepared her breakfast and made up the tray, she had picked up the vase of roses from her office in the next room, thinking she would savor the last blush of the blooms. Instead of fading as all the songs and poems say they do, her roses now seemed to have become more intensely colored. The edges of the petals had darkened and even the rest of the blooms were a darker, deeper, bloodier red color than they were originally. But they were dead, dead as if some very caring person had dried them. She briefly tried to remember the rules for drying fresh flowers. Something about hanging them upside down or laying them in sand, or was it baking soda? But she had not done any of that, and yet they were here, two of them perfectly formed even if drooping and one that had never opened but still upright.

She saw in that one erect rosebud on her tray Sasha's erect penis from the night before, the same size, intensity, and color, swaying ever so slightly as it throbbed. The pale light from the parking lot stanchions cast a pale, soft glow over them both…

She closed her eyes, head back on her pillows and wondered if last night had really happened—if she had in fact let it happen. And as she lay there, the phone rang.

"How are you?" Sasha asked, quietly. "How do you feel?"

"Very fragile—and foolish."

"No need for that. Are you okay?"

"Yes. Just trying to sort through what happened. Are you on a secure phone? With all the Government contracts and secrecy around there, do you know if your calls are monitored? Can we really talk, or...?"

"Well, I can't say for sure, but I don't believe the phones are monitored. Isn't that illegal in this country?"

"Well, of course it's illegal, like lots of other less offensive things we could both think of quickly, but what does that have to do with Government contracts? Your company could probably make a case for monitoring telephone calls of employees in order to maintain national security."

"Perhaps between customers and service reps... Look, it is difficult for me to call you from here—actually, it'll probably be difficult for me to call you very often at all. I want you to know that. That doesn't mean I won't be thinking of you or wanting to see you. Actually, I think about you a lot."

"When?"

"Different times. When I go for my nine o'clock coffee break, like now, I'll be wondering if you're still in bed reading the paper or doing other things in bed..."

"Are you suggesting I might be doing "other things" that some might call lewd and lascivious? Sasha dear, two things: one, if I were, I wouldn't let you know; and two, I really don't have much need for that this particular morning, you know?"

"Suppose I call you some early morning..."

"You are calling me this early morning..."

"But I might call you some morning when I hadn't been with you the night before?"

"And then?"

"I would recall for you all the particular... Would you say you were very kinky?" He pronounced it "keenky."

"I wouldn't say I was kinky at all, if that's a direct question."

"Not even a little bit?"

"…perhaps we need to define kinky…"

"Then tell me what you like and I'll tell you if it's 'keenky' or not."

"Sasha, this conversation is getting too strange for where you are. You don't have this on a speaker phone do you? I have this feeling my words are booming all over the factory floor for entertainment."

"Sweet One, never. Whatever happens between us will always be only between us."

"Well, say something wonderful to me in Croatian then."

"What do you want me to say?"

"You choose. If we weren't on the phone but were together somewhere private, what would you say?"

His words in that exotic, strange-to-her language teased her ears, atingle now with thoughts of his warm breath passing from her ears throughout her body, anticipating the delights that awaited that body, eager to give herself over to him.

"Okay, Sweet One, hang up now."

"No. I don't want to be the first one to hang up."

A moment's pause in which he heard an etude of Chopin's in the background… "What is that music?"

"Chopin…"

A few moments of silence. And then she heard his voice, "Such slow, lovely music. One could start at either end and very slowly move to the other. It would take a long time, Tina, just keeping time with the music, don't you think?"

"If you started at the bottom, would I have to start at the top? And what would happen if the music finished before we finished?"

"Now we have to hang up, or I will soon be embarrassing myself here. Go ahead, hang up."

"But I can't. I want to hear more. Do you want to hear more of the music?"

And she held the phone near the speaker.

"Justina." It was the first time she had heard him pronounce her name—slowly, softly, erotically. "Hang up. Go, now."

"Ummm. I can't be the first to leave. I'll count to three and then you have to promise to hang up. We'll do this together—hang up the phones, that is. Okay? One, two, three." And she gently cradled the phone in the handset, heart beating out of control. With her back arched, she pressed her arms to her sides. She was afraid she would fly apart, be airborne, if she didn't hold herself together.

The Chopin played on, and Justina Lazlo Packard eventually came back to earth. And then she realized she didn't know if he had hung up on the count of three as he had promised.

CHAPTER FIVE

How does one leave all the years of propriety, of doing the right thing, doing the acceptable for some moments of madness and the unknown? Or is it exactly the madness and the unknown which attract after all the years of propriety and appropriateness? She hated that word, appropriate. She had been "appropriate" all her life.

Justina flung herself into an abyss where she wandered aimlessly. What am I doing? Why did I let that happen? Jesus, God, for a few minutes of pleasure I threw away all sense of who I am. And now I don't even know who I am. If I could do that, what other monstrosities am I capable of?

She waited, almost impatiently, for the call from the university. None came. She waited, nervously, for someone to notice some change in her. No one did. She waited, and she waited. But nothing else seemed to have changed. She felt like the last leaf on a tree in late autumn, hanging by that slender stem that binds it to its home, buffeted by the vagaries of pounding rains and thrashing winds, but still it swings—merrily, some times; perilously, at others. But Justina knew the leaf would fall, and she anticipated that the fall would be as disastrous for her as for the leaf—leaving the airy, familiar heights to tumble to the earth, there to be ground to dust by a passing boot or having escaped the footfall, to lie there, unsecured, blown first this way, then that in the Indian Summer, or to feel the tines of the rake snatching at its former dignity and being unceremoniously dumped into the trash. She knew; she knew this what was in store for her.

And coupled with the waiting was a growing anger. If I am this person, this monster, then why haven't I known it before? Why hasn't everyone, anyone else seen it? Is it such perfidy, such treachery to want something else? Even to risk everything? I have taken risks before, but they were all the risks that were acceptable (damn, damn, damn, appropriate) and I always had a safe haven. Now I'm curious and I want to dare—to explore.

But, of course, she couldn't say such things to anyone. She couldn't say, "I am so afraid to die while I am still alive." That was too honest. No one would understand. "But you have everything. What can you mean? Why are you talking like this? Have you gone mad?" Moreover, they really wouldn't want to have to deal with this new Justina. They really liked her the way they thought they knew her, not as she was threatening to become.

As she broke down the pieces of this conundrum she was facing, she tried to do what she had so often suggested to others: One piece at a time. So…

It's not just sex. (But, of course, it was the sex.) I also want to get away from this pretend city. I want to live on the twenty-second (or the thirty-sixth or the forty-seventh) floor of a hi-rise apartment building in the middle of a teeming, dangerous city—alone.

But she knew she'd have to change so much, too much? to do that—hurt so many people, leave them behind, expose herself. And she finally understood that she had spun a fragile web, each filament connected not only to another but to a person she loved, and she saw the web, geometrically perfect and quite beautiful, dew drops sparkling on it in the early morning, the late afternoon sun radiating its trapezoids and parallelograms, never to shine and sparkle quite the same if she disturbed it.

It's my own fault, in a way. I sold myself to everyone as they needed me, and in practicing that deception, without ulterior motives, I think, I abandoned the right to be otherwise. So am I forever obligated to that error in judgment on my part, that kindness? When does it end? Will it? Can it?

She finally admitted to herself that the routine and the safe and secure appealed to her middle class mind and upbringing, but what of her soul?

It's not just the glitz and the glamour and the passion. I long for the investigation—what there is that I don't yet know and how I can learn it. Most of all, after all these years of looking after others, and they are the others I love and have loved, I want to know about myself. Can Sasha teach me something? Or is this the ultimate self-indulgence?

Indeed, who was she, who is she now? She married at nineteen to a man ten years her senior. They were compatible. No major arguments. When she thought about it, there weren't any arguments. Now, she wondered, "How could that be?" They had a very pleasant existence—not numerous highs, and certainly not many lows. The contracts Wil worked on and was awarded, the education she pursued while the children were growing, and now they were off on their own. When she thought of their life together, she summed it up with an incident she never forgot. They were watching a child psychologist on TV one night, and she turned to Wil and said, "What do you think about that?"

"What?" he asked.

"What this doctor is saying about children's role in the family."

"I don't know."

"Well, what do you think about a child's role in the family?"

"To be honest with you, it never occurred to me to think about it. Is something wrong with the kids?"

"No, of course not; but now that it's come up, what do you think?"

"To be honest with you, Justina, I'm probably still not going to think about it."

End of discussion, and Wil got up to refresh his drink. And she thought,

"Well, at least he's honest."

Is there a way to connect with another person—at least in marriage, that legal, socially, religiously inhibiting, self-righteous contract—and still find fulfillment and be honest with yourself? If so, I haven't managed it. I know I draw from that partnership much that I need. But I also know the cost of the valuable deposits I make into to it. And right now I don't think it is an even exchange. Oh, the cost...

But she kept up appearances, met with her classes, consulted with her clients, attended social functions with Wil because that was what Justina did. On the exterior, everything seemed quite ordinary, even to her, except for those exquisite hours when she and Sasha came together.

And in those hours, her guilt vanished entirely and was replaced by awe and the wonder of their magic. She became a precious vessel into which Sasha poured himself to resurrect her—in an ancient, holy ritual performed with reverence and passion and tenderness—invisible but benevolent graces hovering overhead, looking down upon them approvingly, and banishing guilt from their presence.

Sometimes she wondered what Sasha was thinking as they lay there in the peaceful aftermath of their loving, their spent bodies still searching for completion in the other, their very pores exchanging each other's essence— whatever either of them still had left to offer as an additional gift.

They lay there in their bliss, feeling at once vulnerable and complete; absorbing the scent of their mingling; looking into each other's eyes seeing everything clearly and seeing nothing; tasting each other—salty and sweet on their tongues, in their throats; remembering the primitive sound of their climax and hearing the sound of their silence now.

But it was in the silence of those other nights that guilt appeared, unbidden but welcomed in some perverse way by Justina as she wandered the corridors of Hell—mentally pacing, waiting for the first shoe to drop, excoriating herself, and in the morning looking carefully in the mirror to make sure that the whips she had beaten herself with during the night had left no welts that would be visible to others.

CHAPTER SIX

D uring those first few months, Justina imagined some other being had taken possession of her. What did she even see in this young man—the way she referred to him when she was berating herself. She tried being objective. And failed. And in really bad moments, she cursed herself. For Christ's sake. You teach research methodology. Analyze this! Quantify it! And failed.

She could not use research techniques or information from any other course she taught to analyze the effect Sasha had on her. How to quantify the cumulative effect of his kisses, his hands —when she thought about it, where were his hands? She never thought, "Ah, he is touching my breast." But they were all over her body, finding erotic places where she rolled on deodorant, shaved her legs, did all those ordinary morning chores; his fingers probing, gently stroking the most public parts of her body as if they had been hidden all her life. His tongue, gently stroking the backside of her ear, hiding in her navel, finding its way up the inside of her leg until it came to that most private part of her body. And his penis with the rose red tip…

To whom could she send a questionnaire? This was a question only she could answer. But she couldn't. And thinking about it only caused her to forget her analysis; she could feel her passion for him rising, wanting to be with him, having him inside her in the sweet, gentle way he entered her, and when neither one of them could bear another moment, finally demanding her response. Which she was oh, so willing to give.

In her mental meanderings, she grew to know that it could not have been this way with anyone else. And she finally accepted that there was "something" about Sasha that appealed to the more profound side of her—it was more than just the sex. But she never discounted the sex.

The notion that they were similar, searching, ageless peasants finally made her comfortable. Both of us cultivating these fields with their promised fertility but upon which rain falls only when a butterfly spreads its wings in some distant land, or the clouds and winds commune in their own ancient tongue. I can't account for our response otherwise, but we are at different places in our farming and I wonder sadly whether we will help or inhibit each other. When our crop fails, I will analyze the seed I used, the soil, the sun and the rain, seek to know and eagerly embrace the knowing for the next crop. He will shake his fist at the gods of rain and sun and blame himself.

She saw him in herself—looking in a mirror at her own image and seeing him reflected back to her. Absolutists, each of them— she went to the dictionary to make sure that defined them. But no, much as they might aspire to perfection, they realized their own imperfections made patently clear to them. They had only to look into the clear, pure spring water in the pool of their desire to see it muddied by the whirlpools and eddies and turmoil they had created.

She closed her eyes and squeezed them shut tightly—a child making the world disappear—and sank into that sullied pool and lay momentarily in the fine, moist silt at the bottom enjoying the ooze and the dark. When she surfaced, she thought, "No. Idealists— wanting perfection in an imperfect world, unwilling deep down to accept less." But why should they expect the perfection they sought, these two imperfect people? As much as they had betrayed others, they had betrayed themselves. They considered themselves moral, and knew what they were doing was immoral, thumbing their noses at all the values they cherished. But neither one of them had the will to stop—not yet. They would have to wait for perfection.

It was close to midnight and Justina had laid aside the morning paper she was just now reading when she began her reverie. She sighed, and picked up the paper once more. An ad for a concert caught her attention as she turned the page. She rearranged the paper so she could read it—an all Rachmaninov concert. She smiled wickedly to herself; her thoughts of becoming this perfect person vanished quickly.

She purchased two tickets on the aisle, last row balcony, and sent one of them to Sasha at work without a note or any other explanation… She knew that should they be seen together, she could explain it away, but he would despair. Thus, the seats in the last row balcony where no one could sit behind them.

The night of the concert, she selected a long, black moire taffeta suit from her closet. The jacket had four covered buttons close together beginning at the waist and rising up the midriff where the jacket separated into a long slit ending at the throat. Filling the slit were strands of creamy pearls, caught at the base of her throat with a broach. Over the suit she wore a long, black velvet cape with a marabou-trimmed hood that fell into a huge collar down her back. The lobby of the concert hall was papered with floor-to-ceiling mirrors, multiplying the huge bouquets of flowers and the concert crowd—perfumed, well dressed bodies; cultured voices rising and falling amid the sound of genuine and forced laughter; hands holding their pre-concert drinks in plastic cups offered at the bar; men holding their women by the elbow with one hand, coats and wraps draped over their arms; pearls, baubles, real diamonds and fake; real people and fake.

Justina did not know if she would occupy that second seat in from the aisle alone, the aisle seat vacant, or if Sasha would come. She would enjoy the concert either way. She decided to wait until the lights went down and then slip into her seat. If Sasha came, they could both enjoy this evening.…

But for now, she was startled by a hand on her shoulder. Surely, he wouldn't—but the thought was cut short as she turned around to a greeting from a casual acquaintance. "Tina, How nice to see you. Where's Wil? Where are you sitting?"

She smiled, made a moue, and lied. "Oh, he's busy tonight—and I'm up in that rarefied air of the balcony. Someone had a ticket she couldn't use…"

And as she said the words, she saw him! He was handsome as only Sasha could be for her in a dark suit and black leather overcoat. Please God, no white socks, for Sasha was very partial to white socks.

When his then manager had suggested he apply for the job he now had, Sasha was happy to call her with the news. And Justina, trying to be helpful, made a few suggestions on how to conduct himself during the interview.

"Justina, it's not a vice-presidency. It's just a low-level management position."

And he thought then how opposite they were and how good for each other. He kept her grounded with his rather jaded sense of what was real, and she helped him enjoy the potential benefits of any situation. She was always planning for and operating three phases ahead of reality, while he was reluctant to believe the evidence of the here and now. He needed to wait and see. Even with her.

"…and don't wear white socks to the interview."

"Why not? In Europe where hot water and laundry are not so taken for granted as they are in America, white socks are a status symbol. If they are really white—clean—it is evidence that you have access to both the hot water and the laundry facilities."

"But they are not a status symbol here. You're expected to have hot water and access to a laundry. Trust me on this one. Just don't wear white socks to the interview."

And he wondered with a smile what she was thinking when she took off those white socks so lovingly when they undressed each other—but of course I'm not applying for a job with her. He thought, "Is she in a hurry to get to the spaces between his toes or just to get those socks out of her sight?"

She lost the thread of her conversation temporarily but was able to recover, wishing her ersatz companion a good evening's music and excusing herself.

The lobby was slowly emptying of its cargo, but there were still crowds of people between them. He was standing off to a side, leaning against the wall, smiling slightly, knowingly, watching her. How long has he been here?

She looked at him from where she stood, dizzy with the thought of what they were doing—his hands in his coat pockets in a casual way that belied his innate elegance (or did it reinforce that elegance?) and his dark, good looks, his self-possessed carriage, self-assured, and she thought of Heathcliff once again—brooding—in that most magnetic and mysterious way.

They ignored each other, but to Justina it seemed as if a force field had cleared between them in spite of the crush of concert go-ers separating them. She could feel his warmth, his personal scent invading her nostrils over the perfumes that drifted around her, her mouth alternately dry and flowing with the taste of him. She turned away from him deliberately, knowing he watched her, and rounded a corner out of his sight where she could recover. She slipped into the nearest ladies' room and added herself to the ridiculous, anonymous line that is a constant in all theaters.

And then there was that decorous warning bell, and Justina hur-ried to the mini-lobby outside her seating area, waiting to open the door until the lights went down and the polite applause rose up. She took her seat just as the music began, and Sasha took her hand. Rachmaninov's Piano Concerto No, 1 in F Sharp Minor began. And she thought, "This is some kind of perfection—not the thing itself, but close, even if fleeting."

CHAPTER SEVEN

Justina kept hearing Sasha say, "Take off your panties" in her poorly lit car that night. She was still feeling how moonstruck she was on that almost moonless night, wondering what lunacy impelled her to obey him. But the insanity of it only made her smile as she remembered their thrashing about, trying to avoid the console and her stick shift, and she realized that neither of them would be deterred until they joined each other in that euphoria where there was nothing else—only the two of them now made one.

In more rational moments, she thought, "My god, Carter's (or was it Hanes?) cotton panties I've been wearing since I was potty trained." She tried to remember, but couldn't, if she had even bought sexy panties for her honeymoon, and all she could remember was the lovely satin nightgown and peignoir her sister had bought her as a shower present. Oh, yes, and high-heeled white satin mules with satin pom-poms or roses or something on them. She felt sure she hadn't been tuned into sexy underwear at nineteen in the late '50's. Everything was supposed to be so pure and virginal. Sexy stuff would have identified her as more knowledgeable than she was supposed to be at that point. She counted herself a "nice girl." She could remember the desire, the aching when Wil would drive her home, and they would "neck" before she returned to her own bed—alone—but that was a long time ago, literally and now, with their sexuality becoming a memory, figuratively.

But by 1990, even Justina had become aware of the sexual revolution and the rather casual way people talked about, thought about, sex. She had always thought it rather tawdry, but she was "hip" enough to engage in the talk if not the activity—but always in the abstract. "Nice girls"—women—didn't discuss their own sex lives.

And the '60's for Justina had been spent with those same damned Carter's panties only they were her children's. Who had time for communes and drugs and any revolutions when you were responsible for three toddlers?

She smiled now at her naiveté remembering a party she and Wil had been invited to. An artist colleague of Wil's who was really into Jackson Pollack had defiled his beautiful hardwood floors—painted them white and then spatter painted them in pastels and black; his white painter's overalls and the overalls of his gay partner similarly fashioned. Justina was feeling very cosmopolitan and excited in the Bohemian atmosphere. And then at some point during the evening there was some conversation about the brownies someone had brought. Justina was shocked and quietly approached Wil, wine glass in hand, and whispered that they'd better go. Will was having a good time, too, and said, "In a few minutes." But Justina, anticipating a police raid at any moment—she could already envisage the mug shots of them pinned up in the post office—insisted they leave, finally hissing quietly in Wil's ear, "There's marijuana in the brownies." They left as soon as it was polite to go.

And here she was—contemplating what?

For now a shopping trip…

First, some expensive panty hose. After that first night in the car, Justina took a good, long look at herself in her mirror. She's have to lose a few pounds—maybe there was a reason the elastic on her panties was slightly stretched? How long was it since she stepped on a scale? Whatever…here she was, looking at the cellulite that had accumulated on her thighs—the unavoidable sign of aging. She knew she couldn't get rid of it, so the quest for the new pantyhose—lace tops, nude shades, and of course, black. Hide it!

She hit the most expensive store in town, passing the cosmetics and perfume counters—later—and headed straight for the lingerie aisles. She was on a mission to make manifest this new-found sensuality she had discovered. She could feel the comfortable cotton engirding her nether regions, her hips, all the way up her waist, washed and dried a hundred times. In her mind she could see that elastic, a bit stretched and loose, the bindings around the legs, shabby and worn—not yet torn or raggedy, no strings or threads hanging from the edges, just eroding quietly away with each laundering. "Probably a bit gray if I really looked," she thought sadly, ashamed; then laughed as she remembered Sasha's white socks...

Justina fingered the lovely silk things in the delicious, pale colors. "All those disgusting worms, chewing away on mulberry leaves, for this!" she thought. "Such an irony." Then, mockingly, "My cotton panties are almost as fine a year, two years later, washed to a fine gauze. But it's a dingy, gray gauze," she reminded herself. "God, when was the last time I bought any underwear?"

She looked at any array of panties with matching bras, most of them bikinis and some strange things with a band up the back side. They didn't look very comfortable. Even in this luscious pastel silk they reminded her of chastity belts from some ancient, tortured century.

She tried first one bra, then the next, and the rest, deciding on two that seemed to flatter her and were the most comfortable. She was getting dressed when the sales clerk (Mona—she had seen her name tag) knocked softly on the door. "Can I get you anything else?"

Justina opened the door. "No, thanks. I've made up my mind. Here, I'll take these, but I'll want several, so I'll have to come out to choose the colors," and she handed off the two she wanted into Mona's outstretched hand, and then into her other hand, the rest of them.

Mona smiled, conspiratorially, "New man in your life?"

Justina halted in her final efforts to get dressed and turned. "Why would you ask that?"

"Well, forgive me, but when we have a woman come in here who has decided to buy a whole new underwear wardrobe, that's what it usually means. Most women usually come in to buy one or two replacements at a time... Sorry, I didn't mean to be offensive. You just looked sort of, I don't know—dreamy and happy—like there could be a new man. And I saw you looking at nighties and robes and things…" Her voice trailed off, and she smiled, apologetic and shy, yet coy.

Justina slithered into her suit jacket. "I just decided that now was the time to treat myself to all this." And they walked back onto the sales floor together, now "sisters" by way of this strange rite of buying intimate apparel.

Justina, still looking through the panties, picked up the "chastity belt" thing, and said, "This does not look very comfortable."

"Oh, the thong. It's been around for a while. I tried one, and I didn't like it, but some women say it's the most comfortable thing they've ever worn." Justina held up a pair of panties that looked like the mini-est of mini skirts., flared and ruffled, low cut like a bikini. "How the hell do you get your panty hose over that?"

Mona laughed. "I think those are just for play, if you know what I mean."

The pile of pale rainbow colors—pink, blue, green, aqua, apricot—panties grew, and Justina selected her two bra styles in matching colors. "I think that will do it for today." And then on impulse, she said, "I think I'll take one of these as well," and held up the pair of panties that were "for play." "The apricot ones."

Mona raised her eyebrows but said nothing, just smiled. Then, "Since you're treating yourself, there are some lovely nighties and robes on sale over here. Why don't you just take a look?"

And Justina allowed herself to be led away, noticing a separate counter of lipstick red lace things, naughty-looking things, that could also be had in black or white. "Enough, already," she cautioned herself.

She selected a long, white silk kimono which was on sale—30 per cent off, but still incredibly expensive—half the price of a good suit. "Not to worry, darling," she chided herself, "You can afford it."

Mona was now busy toting up the sale, gently folding these precious items one by one and wrapping them in lavender tissue. When Justina got them home and unwrapped them, she realized the tissue was lavender scented, but now she just handed over her credit card, and Mona laid everything into a white, shiny square box.

Justina was signing the bill when Mona said, "Well, whoever he is, I hope he appreciates this."

CHAPTER EIGHT

They had ordered their drinks, and Maggie sat there peeling the petals off the rose bud, sipping her martini. Maggie was her own woman; she didn't "do" wine when every other woman in the world seemed to be drinking White Zin. She looked Justina straight in the eye and said, rather bitterly, "Wives still belong to husbands in the most ancient way." Several more petals fluttered down onto the starched white linen.

Justina was silent and thought, "This is going to be some evening."

Maggie continued. "It's all a myth. Women's lib, all that shit. It just became fuckingly more complicated than it used to be."

There had been a vase of coral roses on the table when Justina arrived. Now there was one less in the vase, and Justina idly wondered if it would be added to their bill. Maggie was the friend and business colleague of one of Justina's best friends. They knew each other casually and had met at several wine and cheese things and other social events. They hadn't seen each other for a few months until Justina passed Maggie a few days before in the hospital where she works. Justina had contracted to provide some training sessions to new employees. They made a date right then for dinner and this was the evening.

Maggie was a short, almost dumpy woman, not fat, but once Justina had asked her when the baby was due because she knew Maggie was trying to get pregnant and thought she had been successful. She was not pregnant then. But she must have forgiven Justina for her insensitivity because they remained casual friends—not best friends. She was pretty in the way of an Irish colleen, which in fact she was. She was married to a man whom most of her friends considered hostile, but he turned out to be silent instead. Not at all the same thing, but often pretty close to the same thing. Justina was always a bit put off by him, wondering what secrets he harbored. Maggie was effervescent and had a wonderful smile, marred by teeth that still needed the attention they had never gotten when she was pre-pubescent.

Justina had been thinking about these impressions of Maggie since she had passed her in the hall a few days earlier because she had been stunned, barely recognizing her.

Here was Maggie leaving the hospital to go home. She wore a short denim skirt with running shoes and socks and looked about fourteen years old. She was tiny—petite, slim and adorable. Probably the reason she agreed to make a definite dinner date with Justina then was that the first uncontrolled words out of Justina's mouth on recognizing her were, "My God, Maggie, who's the man?"

Maggie stood rooted where she was, totally taken aback, then recovered and laughed gaily. "How did you know?"

"Umm, nothing in a woman's life makes her look like you do except sex with a wonderful man—probably a new man, since regular sexual partners like husbands don't ususaly change enough to precipitate such change."

Maggie laughed again, and said, "Let's have dinner—lunch won't be long enough."

So here they were at the Ritz, the de riguer "in" place, and she was about to begin her story.

"I still can't believe you saw it right off."

"Well I haven't seen you for several months, so the change was striking."

"Isn't it funny? David hasn't noticed a thing—still doesn't suspect anything has changed." She glanced off into the distance.

"Yes, but in all fairness, when you see someone every day, the changes are subtle and less noticeable." Justina leaned across the table, "So, tell me…"

"Well, he's someone I work with and it's just so plain and simply wonderful! I can't believe it; moreover, I can't believe I'm telling anyone about it." She sipped at her martini. "Thanks, Justina, there is some relief in the telling. You know, I can't confide in anyone at work—and it's seems like too much of a betrayal to talk about it with any close friends of ours—David's and mine—so you're just right!" She laughed softly. "Would you believe I've never until now had sex in the back seat of a car—or out of doors—or been to a football game—held hands at a concert? I feel sixteen." She smiled, and Justina realized she was no longer aware of her crooked teeth. Aha! She had had them fixed. And Justina wondered, amused, whether she, too, had bought new underwear.

The waiter came to take their orders, and left. Justina noticed that he did not remove the small pile of rose petals near Maggie's almost empty martini glass, merely asked, "Would you like to refresh your drinks?" They both nodded in the affirmative. Justina thought, "Yes, indeed. We both need another one."

Maggie's flash of bitterness was gone, thoughtfulness replacing it. She began on a second rose, tenderly removing the petals and arranging them in a circular pattern that spiraled outward from a center she had arranged.

"One of the things I'm learning is the different ways men and women think," she said. "The thing I notice most is that men think in terms of boxes with secure lids and women think in terms of circles intersecting and overlapping with fuzzy limits.

"David, for instance, has put me and Steven into this rather smallish box marked, 'Wife and Child,' and not only tightly secured the lid but locked it to make sure nothing unusual gets in and certainly that we could never get out. I'm not saying that I didn't enjoy that box for a while. But here it is, 1992, I'm a hospital administrator, I earn a lot of money, I do more than I ever expected to do, but I feel as if I'm living in 1950—or 1850. Once you're in that box, 'Wife and Mother,' the only way you ever get to see any other side of your real self is by breaking open the box and escaping."

Their drinks had arrived, and just in time.

"Everything in our society encourages us to stay there. Every system, every institution has been designed subtly or blatantly to keep it that way. It doesn't even matter that I'm one of the few executive women in a male-dominated profession...

"Sometimes my scalp hurts as I imagine myself being dragged through history by my hair—you know, the way cartoons depict cave men and women." She sipped at her martini slowly and examined the spiral of rose petals. Quickly, with a wave of her hand she created disarray and began re-arranging them.

"It's not that I don't love David, and of course, I worry constantly about Steven. David and I live well together. We probably need to stay together for all the reasons we married in the first place. But we're just two entirely different people today who share the same adult history. We were both young when we married and our whole adult lives have been spent together. We both adore Steven. David probably loves me to the extent he can and as best as he knows how. It's just not enough..." The last was melancholy and plaintive.

She had arranged the rose petals now in three intersecting circles. "See? here I am in the middle. I'm willing, even eager to share this area," she paused while she filled the elliptical area formed by the intersection of two of the circles with additional rose petals, "with David. That's about how our lives intersect, in fact. But, Justina, just look at what's left over!"

She began filling the other ellipse where her circle and the third intersected. "Gary gives life to this other part of me. In truth, if it weren't for him," she began rearranging the first filled area to make it smaller, "there would be so much less for David. Does that make any sense to you?"

The waiter appeared with their salads and waited while Maggie swept up the rose petals and dropped them in the ash try. As the waiter left, Maggie picked up her fork, held it in the air for a moment, and asked, "Do you think I'm weird, or what? Maybe deep down I'm just a slut."

Justina hadn't yet picked up her fork. "My God, no. I understand completely. It's really peculiar that you use the analogies of the boxes and circles. You see, I am involved with another man, too—but that's another dinner.

"When it began, I was filled with guilt and the craziness of what

I was doing. And as you well know, you can't turn to your mother for advice on this one. Always before I turned to Wil; even when he couldn't resolve my problem, just saying hearing myself say the words usually brought me to some further place. However, this was not a topic I was going to share with him." They both laughed. "Although it is strange that on at least three different occasions I have come close to doing just that. I've backed away because of the caveman principle you described earlier. Even though sex is nonexistent in our marriage and Wil is open and broad-minded—once he told me that if I needed to, I could have an affair. Imagine!—but he still needs to be married to me. He's not good at dissembling and I always end up wondering exactly what would be gained. Every time I was out of his sight, I know he would be wondering if I was with 'that man.' I guess the only thing gained would be my relief from not having to sneak around.

"Mind you, I am no longer guilty—well, not much, about my love for Sasha, my guy—Hell, I'm still not sure it isn't pure lust—but I despise the fact that I have to invent reasons to be gone and that they are lies. There's also the risk of being caught. Perhaps that why the French, bless them, invented (or at least gave a name to) the menage a trois. If that's not exactly what we're after, at least it's closer… And it would be honest and I long for that honesty.

"Anyway, back to the boxes. Do you remember Jorge Lopez, the city councilman? We've been good buddies ever since I worked on that inner city project. He is a charming, married roué, and I always assumed his wife knew of his sexual adventures because everyone else seemed to. In fact our names were linked together by many who knew us both because he laid everything that wore a skirt. Actually, he never even made a pass at me—once I asked him why, and he said, 'Mother Superior? For that I'd surely burn in hell.'—but we've stayed in touch and lunch together every once in a while.

"Anyway, when this thing with Sasha first began, he was the person I trusted to ask how he had managed to stay aloft all these years. He, too, referred to boxes—said he puts his liaisons into little boxes and shelves them. They never interfere with any other part of his life, and if and when they do, he runs. Leaves that box on the shelf and never opens it again… finds a new box to fill and play in…"

"Sounds about right from my observations, but Justina, I can't believe you…" Maggie's voice trailed off. "Everybody thinks you have the perfect marriage. Yours is the standard by which the rest of us measure our own."

She was silent as the waiter brought their meals. "So, what it all comes down to is no one knows what goes on—or doesn't go on—behind closed doors."

Justina pushed some of the food around on her plate. "Funny," she mused, "I never used anyone's marriage as a guide for mine. But Wil and I have changed—in different ways—Wil seems content to shrink from the unknown at the same time I'm eager to embrace it. Maybe it's a function of the differences in our ages. Have you read Gail Sheehy's *Passages*? And maybe, certainly, it's the effects of all the drugs he now has to take after his by-pass surgery. I thank God every day that I've had the freedom I've had and that Wil is used to my independence professionally and socially, left over from when I was that faithful wife.

"But we agreed that tonight was your story. We'll do mine another time. I'll just say this, Maggie. I can't know how your Gary has affected or influenced you. I can only wish for you—and I'd guess it's so from looking at you—that whatever is going on between you has given you back to yourself, do you know what I mean? I know I am so grateful to Sasha every single day. If I were never to see him again, never to touch him, have sex with him, I would weep, be inconsolably sorry, but amidst that pain and longing, I'd be eternally, everlastingly grateful. I know my own body now.

"It's as if for the first time I am acquainted with the carapace that houses the real me—I feel like a turtle that has escaped from its moorings and is free to roam about on top of her shell, touching all the hitherto unknown places she couldn't reach and finding them all beautiful to savor—such a new vision of myself and the world, smelling all the aromas that are me—I can recreate them in my head at will—the smell of Sasha; his taste, the thought of him makes my mouth water—as well as a few other places." They giggled.

Maggie nodded. "I know. It's like being born again as an adult.

I try to remember if this is how I felt when I was first in love with David. I remember thinking it was heaven at the time, but first sex and first love are two entirely different things, don't you think? I remember the love part differently from the sex part. Actually, I think first sex is educational more often than erotic. By the time you get around to it and with all the fears and anxieties, it's less enjoyment than achievement.

"With Gary, it's all erotic and delightful. The anxiety isn't in the sex, but in the risk, and that soon vanishes with the pleasure. I guess the down side is the things that go 'bump' in the night. The unexpected phone call when no one is supposed to know where either of us is, and it turns out to be the desk making sure we're happy with our room; or the knock at the door and it's someone with half a bag on who's looking for 2014 and we're in 2041. Probably the worst thing I ever did early on was to leave an expensive bottle of perfume behind in the bathroom. I had actually booked the room in my own name and charged it to my account. I know. I know." That last in response to Justina's rolling her eyes. "But I'm telling you this was early on, and I was trying to avoid lying as much as possible. I told myself I had the right to check into a hotel for an afternoon if I wanted to, and furthermore David never opened my mail nor paid my bills so it was safe.

"I was glad to let the perfume go—I prayed some maid slipped it into her pocket, but for weeks I lived in fear of arriving home to find the package with 'Hilton Hotels' on it and having to explain to David how I happened to be staying at a local Hilton Hotel. Thank God for that little bit of dishonesty among the chambermaids. If I could have found her, I would have tipped her handsomely."

They were finishing their dinners, and Maggie continued with her story. By the time their coffees arrived, Justina wondered how many more women there were out there with similar tales. Just when they think they have it all—marriage, family, professional success, they realize they've been shrink-wrapped, very properly packaged and labeled, and hung on one of those hooks in an ordinary variety store. If you turned the package over to look at the ingredients, you'd find the joys and fears, the successes and disappointments, the children and the husbands, the work and the play, and perhaps even the lovers would be listed. But like any list, the totality was very different from the individual parts.

The bill came with the requisite chocolate mints on the tray. They each looked at it, agreed to add 25 percent (They were each conscious of the fact that women were considered poor tippers and so over-compensated.) and laid their individual credit cards on the tray. Justina snickered. "Can you imagine our mothers having such a dinner—$100 plus just to kvetch with a friend?"

Maggie rolled her eyes. Justina continued, "And in spite of the fact that we're each madly, euphorically in love, we've just spent the better part of two hours bitchin' about how tough the world is. Maggie, you and I, we know a whole bunch of women like us—we make a lot of money, we seem to 'have it all.' But it's never enough, is it? The more we have, the more we think we deserve—or at least want."

"Yeah, I know. It's what keeps me awake at night—at least the nights I'm not with Gary. Those nights I just don't give a damn. I'm damned sure I deserve it all." And Maggie pushed back her chair. They unhooked their designer bags from the backs of their chairs and left the restaurant.

As Justina climbed into her car, she remembered a psychologist at a seminar when women were still not so popular at professional gatherings. They had exchanged small talk and he eventually began to talk about his children. She thought at the time, to let her know he was married. Finally, he asked if she had any children, and when she replied, three and gave their ages, he refused to believe her. Finally, to cover his discomfiture, he offered, "Well, you certainly don't look like a mother."

"Oh," she wondered, "How does a mother look?"

"Well, just not like you."

And there she went, into his box. Now she had a label!

CHAPTER NINE

The sound of the first shoe dropping finally came in the way of a phone message from the Vice-president of Faculty.

"Hi, Justina. It's Kate. Can we get together tomorrow at about ten? We have something we need to discuss. Okay? See you then unless you can't make it. Then call me."

She was so rattled that on her way there, she almost missed the exit off the freeway, carelessly cutting off a driver in the right lane. She was numb; and she barely even heard the long, loud, angry blast of his horn. Ordinarily she would have been chagrined at such driving, but she was somewhere else this morning and it didn't even register.

The nights in her personal Hell had prepared her for this; she had played out all the scenarios, the disgrace, but still coming face to face with it on this sunny day was another rendering. She couldn't think of a single thing to say in her defense. There was nothing to say. She had violated everything she had always held dear—her standards, her ethics, her loyalty to Wil and to the university. Nothing anyone could say would make her feel worse, but she knew public exposure was a different kind of burden.

And now here she was, sitting in the office of the Vice-president—not an unusual occurrence, for they were simpatico on most issues and they were friends. But she knew her affair with Sasha would not be one of those things that Kate could deal with lightly— nor should she, thought Justina. Not that Kate would care whether Justina had an affair or not (although she'd like to know all the details). In fact Kate had confided in Justina when she was in the midst of an affair two years ago, but that was over, and Justina wondered how and if her then rather cavalier attitude about it had caused her to change. Was she bitter? Nothing like a convert to rant and rave against one's own prior missteps when newly found in another. And besides, Kate hadn't had an affair with a student—it was a colleague. And she silently added, "Not one who was twenty years her junior."

Justina wondered whether all workplaces were as incestuous as theirs was. One of the other vice-presidents had, in fact, married a student after divorcing his wife, but she had never been his student in the classroom. Probably learned a lot from him, since she was in her mid twenties and he was pushing fifty. But that was another story, and Justina knew it did not justify her own behavior, nor did the differences in their ages even raise an eyebrow. But a younger woman and an older man were "acceptable." And there were countless rumors with the probability that many of them were more than that.

"You know, we haven't had much time together lately, and we need to catch up," Kate began, and Justina knew she was holding her breath, hoping only that it didn't show. She mentally tried a few different faces—pleasant and normal, neutral but interested, but to her, her face felt frozen. "Do you want to go to lunch?"

"I'd like to do lunch, but not today, I'm already booked. The reason I haven't been around is my own business has taken off and I'm a lot busier than I used to be. That's why I've cut back on my classes here." She attempted a knowing smile as she continued, "You've got to know, there's more money out there than there is here."

"Yeah—well, we're working on a pay increase for faculty, but that's not why I asked you to come in."

Here it comes. Justina shifted in her seat, feeling feverish yet faint.

"Remember when you agreed to sit on the committee to judge the business research projects for the Bowers Award—when was that—more than a year ago? I know, it didn't go anywhere, and we all thought it was just another one of those things that was going to fall through the cracks. But, hear this! It's going to happen this year." And Kate gave a thumbs up. Justina exhaled internally. "The university has sent out letters to all the companies who have graduating seniors to determine which company has benefitted the most from those projects, and the Selection Committee has identified eight projects to be judged.

"It almost doesn't matter who wins, except, I guess to the student and his or her own company, but it's going to get us some great publicity because the response from the business community has been overwhelming. You won't believe the kudos…"

"Great," Justina relaxed, her palms were still sweaty, but her earlier racing heart was returning to normal. It no longer felt as if it would burst from her chest. "So when does this judging of Mr. or Ms. America take place?"

"Well, because of the time involved, we've copied all eight of the projects and the letters from their companies. We're going to distribute them to each of the five judges. I know, I know, a lot of trees and more donation of your time, but it's for a good cause." She smiled, pleadingly. "You just said you were cutting back, but come on, you agreed to do this. The committee is scheduled to meet on March twenty-seventh, so you can squeeze in the reading between now and then. You are going to have to agree on number one by April fifteenth, so we can have the award engraved, and get the information to the printer for the graduation programs."

Thoughts of going through eight research projects was daunting, but she thought, "I won't have to grade them, and presumably, they're all great papers."

Kate was already pushing a stack of papers across her desk toward Justina.

When she saw the master list with its titles and the students' names, she recoiled.

"But I can't be a judge. Two of these are my students!" She almost hissed, And one of them is much more than that to me, she thought in terror. Her heart was beginning to resume its former unnatural cadence.

"Of course, all five judges are research project professors. Who better to judge?"

"But doesn't that create a conflict of interest? Won't there be the aroma of any one of us voting for our own student? This doesn't have the right feel for me…"

"But Justina, that was the agreement of the original committee and Paul Bowers. What do the rest of us know about the process?"

"You can see the results, read the letters from the students' companies….when I agreed to be a judge, it didn't even occur to me that any of my students' papers would be on the short list."

"Justina, everyone else is comfortable with the process. No one thinks any one would vote for a student simply because he or she was theirs… You all grade papers every day on the basis of their worth. What's the big deal?"

Justina was silent. Then, "I'm going to have to recuse myself."

"Why, for heaven's sake?"

"I just told you, Kate. It doesn't feel right to me."

"Which are your students? Did you have a problem with one of them?"

"Alexander What's-his-name—he's called Sasha—" she hoped that in saying Sasha's formal name she didn't betray herself, "and Donna Martin; and no, I didn't have any problems with either one of them. I've been to a party at Donna's house that she had for what she called "favorite faculty" when she finished her last class. She was a temporary drop-out a year ago, and then came back in to finish up this year, so she finished early."

"But everyone does that—goes to students' affairs when they're invited."

"Kate, I can't." Now it was Justina who was plaintive.

They sat silently for a few moments, and suddenly there was a glimmer of understanding in Kate's eyes. "It's the Alexander person, isn't it?"

"Kate, why pursue this? Please just replace me."

"Justina Packard, if I didn't know you better, I'd think you had something going on."

Justina, feeling not at all like being coy, coyly said, "Oh, sure. You want to know the details of this hot and heavy affair I'm having with a student young enough to be my son? Come on, Kate. You know me well enough to know that's not it." Lying some more, she thought.

"Well, I know you well enough to know if… if that were the case you'd be sitting here with me now, saying exactly what you're saying."

"Okay, if you want to find me guilty, I'm guilty…" Justina raised her arms as if being arrested, trying a bravado she didn't feel. "Only there are other reasons why I'm sitting here with you now, saying exactly what I'm saying.

"When I agreed to do this, I really didn't consider that my own students would be candidates. Foolish, I know now. How could it be otherwise? Or at least the chances were great that that's how it would be. To be perfectly frank with you, Kate, I didn't give it a thought—thought we'd be first or second readers or something. And frankly, I hadn't seen any of my own students' projects that looked like winners to me for a long time. But you said yourself this is going to garner some publicity for the university, and I strongly recommend you re-think who the judges are.

"Besides, there's another aspect to Donna Martin. I'm in the process of negotiating a large training contract with her company. Don't you see how impossible all that makes this? It's not in Government contracts which is her department, but still…" She paused.

"That's one of the really big conflicts I have working for the university now—how much of who I know and who knows me is the result of contacts here?"

"Oh, for God's sake, Justina. You have to be employed in your area to even get hired here as adjunct faculty. It's one of our major selling points to the students." And Kate adopted a TV announcer's voice over, "And do you know that all of your instructors will be people who own their own businesses or work for major companies, so you can be assured you will be taught by people who know the workplace."

"Yeah," Justina, finished with her own parody, "only some of them don't know how to teach…" she sing-songed.

"Okay, so who's in your sights now?" Kate sighed.

"No one—just my never-ending pursuit of excellence, my dear." Justina moved, as if to go, eager to leave.

But Kate wasn't finished with her. "Wait. Somehow I want to return to this Alexander—what did you call him? Sasha?"

"Why?" Justina could feel her face freezing again.

"Just because you don't want to... Are you having an affair with him?"

"Oh, for God's sakes, Kate. What do you expect me to say? It's just so ridiculous! How about if I take the Fifth? But that won't satisfy you, because now you're going to be thinking, why couldn't she just say, 'No?'"

"Well, I'm not going to say 'No;' I'm going to leave you thinking your lewd thoughts." And Justina now very deliberately picked up her things, pushed her chair away, and sailed from the office.

CHAPTER TEN

Sasha was waiting for her at "their" place—a motel where they had been meeting set back off the highway but convenient for both of them. Usually, she was early, but after her meeting with Kate, she was caught in traffic.

They had agreed to meet this afternoon, and Justina hadn't told Sasha that Kate had asked to see her, fearing what she had been anticipating. And now she couldn't. So she had to keep this knowledge of his being a candidate for the first Paul Bowers Award to herself. Still, it felt as if it were some kind of betrayal to add to her growing list of lies and betrayals—a secret, and she didn't want to have secrets from Sasha.

But that mood didn't last long. Sasha was standing at the window, staring out into space, when she approached, and immediately opened the door.

"I wasn't sure you would come…"

"But I said I would…"

"I know. It's just that between the time we make a date, and both of us actually get here, I'm always nervous that something will happen. Never mind." He drew her into the circle of his arms, and they stayed together savoring each other's breath; their bodies, fully clothed feeling the heat of their desire. "I'm never sure of you at all."

"Sasha, this isn't easy for either of us." Justina moved slightly to look up into his old-copper eyes. "I think that we are both basically moral people doing something that we both know is immoral." She could see the hurt in those eyes. "Come on, it is immoral, however

we choose to rationalize it to ourselves or to each other. Let's just
hope we have time to repent before we die—the last rites, the last
confession, or whatever."

She sat on the chair. "What do you suppose God thinks of us?
Isn't there a contradiction with a God who gives us the capacity for
joy and then wants to deny us the opportunities to experience it? If
I were God and had created heaven, I wouldn't let anyone in who
hadn't found joy on earth, hadn't found others to share it with. I'd
keep sending them back until they learned the lesson: it is not pain
but joy you are to learn below.

"And if there is no God, no heaven, how much worse to deny
whatever joy is possible here on earth.

"It's not as if I haven't driven myself crazy thinking about it, but
then I think 'How to repair it?' and the answer is not to see you, and
right now, I can't do that either—oh, I guess I could if you didn't
want to see me, but the truth is, I don't want to."

He whispered something in Croatian in her ear.

"Was that something nice or something 'keenky', or…"

"I just said 'You talk too much,' so come here," and he gently
pulled her up out of the chair and moved toward the bed. He unbuttoned her jacket and laid it on the chair, then unzipped her skirt
and laid that on top. She was busy unbuttoning his shirt and unzip-
ping his trousers and feeling his kisses, his wet tongue and his warm
breath on her neck. He pulled back the bed spread and blankets, and
they sat on the edge of the bed, half clothed, half naked, and just
looked at each other—for a long time.

They shed the rest of their clothes as they held their gaze, he,
not looking at her naked body; she, not looking at his erect penis.
Neither of them really cared about the condition of their underwear,
although Justina had worn one of her expensive silk panties and
a matching bra. Sasha did not notice or if he did, made no comment.

"Come with me. Let's shower and wash away your cares, my
sweet one—I want to find your joy for you."

Justina looked at him, questioningly. "You can really do that?"

"You know I can… But I'll have to search all over your body

to make sure I don't miss it because I know it's hiding there some-place…"

She followed him into the shower where Sasha's gentle hands cast his spell over her. She felt safe and secure and pure in his wet, soapy arms as the cascade of cleansing, warm water rained down upon their naked bodies. And she thought they were like children playing in a summer downpour. She felt just like that—innocent and untouched by the world outside.

"Come, lay with me," he whispered as they dried each other.

"Lie with me," she corrected as they got into bed.

"What?"

"Lie with me."

"What do you mean? I don't want to lie to you."

"No, no. The correct verb is "lie" when you want someone to be next to you in bed like this."

"But lie means to tell untruths…"

"Yes, but that's a different verb. People "lie down" when they are doing what we're doing. They "lay" something down."

"That's what I meant. I want to lay you down and fuck you silly." He blew into her ear.

She laughed, "You can lay me down and fuck me silly, Sasha. But I will lie here alongside you."

He sat up. "So what of your wonderful American verbs do you use to tell fibs? Isn't that to lie?"

And as his question hit her, she realized she would lie with Sasha for as long as she could, and she would lie to the rest of world about it. For now, she just wanted him to lay her.

CHAPTER ELEVEN

Each of the men had a dead, red rose bud on the front of his robe. Justina knew what that rose bud represented, and she was cold and afraid. Who were they and why were they here? The men wore long, matte black robes and matching pointed hoods like the Ku Klux Klan. They marched, faceless under those hoods, in the shape of a cross, four down and three across, their robes making the swishing noise of taffeta as they marched toward her. She had a fleeting vision of a black taffeta dress she had worn one night to meet Sasha for an evening of lovemaking. Love was not on her mind right now, but she knew Sasha and her love had precipitated this macabre parade.

She was paralyzed with fear. She was standing in her living room, but in the way of dreams, everyone was out in an open field. The sun was shining, but the sense of death, gloomy yet expectant and reverent, hung about. Lining the sides of the living room cum meadow, it seemed were all the people she had known. She had forgotten how many people had touched her life and she, theirs, but they all seemed to be there and she recognized the faces of many whose names she could hardly remember. Standing back away from these people were the hangers-on, the curious who had come for the show. She backed away, but still they came, slowly, inexorably. As she pressed back, looking for the wall as a support, she realized the space just increased. She stopped and waited.

Some bastardized version of "Pomp and Circumstance" was the only sound heard over the rustle of their robes, no footfalls, no clanging swords at their sides. There was silence from the crowd.

"Pomp and Circumstance?" she screamed, but her voice was still. Pain makes no sound.

So she waited. Would she be burned? She glanced down to see if she had suddenly been branded with a red "A" on her chest, but no. This was 1992; adulteresses were not burned at the stake. "Seventy percent of all married women have had an affair," she shouted. And even as she said it, she knew it had nothing to do with her, with her passion for Sasha, so why was she trying to use these stupid statistics to excuse herself.

Silence.

Then, gently kindly, the two robed figures who had made the arms of the cross stepped forward and took her to their leader. They were now marching back the way they had come. Justina was at the head of this unit, unable to stop, unable to run away. She kept marching to the beat of the insane music. "Pomp and Circumstance," the academician's theme song which could move her to tears in real life, altered to sound like the drumming out of a soldier who was disgraced.

And her life passed before her eyes as she marched to she knew not what:

Wonderful days of childhood, gritty in her own sweat and unaware of her smell. Classrooms where she was both student and teacher—the smell of chalk dust. And the productive days of adulthood; focused on husband, children and later on aging parents. And there she was in bed with Sasha, the sheets rumpled, facing him, their eyes locked in their pleasure and the sweet agony of his rhythmic movement inside her. "For those few times of pleasure, all the rest is overlooked?" she cried, but again, no sound came from her, only the slow, measured beat of the music and the rustle of the robes.

They slowed in front of Sasha, his bearded face so dear to her. She remembered the night of the black taffeta dress when she thought that pleasure would endure forever, whether they ever met again or not. Would he rescue her now? Could he?

He looked into her eyes. Was it disgust or pain? She could not tell. He wanted to be elsewhere. As they passed, she turned once more to plead with him. But he had already left. A cheap looking young woman with an ample ass packed in tight jeans stepped out of the crowd to join him. Justina noticed with satisfaction that her underpants line was showing. So fitting and so tacky, she thought—a new box.

On the other side of the parade route was Wil. Would he defend her? Could he defend her? What would he say? Nothing. He stared down at the ground, and she saw the tear and the quiver of his chin, but he, too, was silent.

Her children stood together. Her daughter shielded her young ones with her skirt, as if she could protect them from the reality of their genes. Her back was to Justina as she passed. "Ah, the days of your childhood, when you were the child and I, the protector." Justina hoped she would have enough time to figure out what motherhood was really all about. Maybe she could still pass on that knowledge to this young mother whom she loved so dearly. Would she be able to accept such a gift from such a mother? And the silence endured as did the march—the space seeming never to decrease—just the music and the rustle of the robes.

Her son knelt as she passed and extended his hand as if in supplication. "What unfinished business have we yet to do?" she wondered. He wept openly. "Does he need me to be someone else to preserve his image of me?"

She knew then that no one could help; perhaps no one even wanted to, but it would have been useless. She was doomed and her fate sealed.

Her best friend looked crossly at her as she passed. She was the spokesperson for all women, Justina knew. "You had more than most of us—a husband who came home every night; he loved you. He didn't carouse; he had no other woman. He was faithful to you."

Justina tried to protest, "But I thought you were my friend. I thought you loved me."

"You wanted too much. You wanted it all. No one else got everything; why should you? Who did you think you were?"

Justina protested, "I wanted to be honest, but none of you would have liked it."

How could it be, Justina thought in her pain and fear, that she had listened to all their stories, their complaints, never passed judgment, yet still valued them as individuals? She knew she could never stand in their places, to know how it really was for any one of them. She had always assumed that they were capable of making mistakes as she knew she was, but that mistakes as the world defines them are not always sins—sometimes they are side roads on the path to knowledge. "Should I have known that there is only one right way for everyone? That everyone else led this same life I led and was therefore eligible to judge me?" She knew that was not it, but she had more than her share of the usual twelve who were willing to stand in judgment.

Her male friends also stood in a group. "We wanted you. You cheated us by keeping us as friends when in fact you were having sex with that immigrant! You always played the part of the satisfied wife so none of us would pursue you. And because we honored and respected you and the fact that you were married, we lost out on the good stuff. You were a fraud!"

She finally understood there was no way she could have won, whether she held herself up to the world as they wanted or if she pursued her own goals. Whatever… She was condemned.

No words had been spoken, yet she heard all this. What had happened before she arrived? Had she been tried in absentia? Of course, this is how judgment is passed every hour of every day on others.

Were straws passed among the crowd? Black for guilt, white for innocence? But they weren't electing a damned pope! Indeed, the black robed leader did not carry any white straws in his hand, only a bundle of black straws. Yes, guilty. Of course, guilty.

Suddenly from the precipice toward which they marched, there was a scream, which stopped the music. The echo of the scream hung in the air. The sun disappeared behind a cloud. A salty mist of delicate tears fell like a veil on her face and her youngest child's screams resumed. From far down in this chasm, where she now knew she would be thrown, this young woman shouted.

"She was never one of you. You all took what you needed from her, as I did. But not one of you gave her the gift she gave you—permission to be herself.

"Her only guilt was in not letting you know who she really was, and so long as she performed to your expectations, you all loved and cherished her. But she was a maverick, born into a society that loved conformity. She tried to be all things to all of you. But that is not who she was. Not one of you lived her life. What do you know?

"Loving Sasha was an effort to figure out who she was, to grow in ways she had never attempted before. She loved him…"

The music started up again and drowned out the last of her words. But still they echoed over the music. "She would not be here. She would not be here to judge any one of you whom she loved, but only to defend you. Go home and leave her alone."

But the group composed its collective steely face, and the unit leader thrust his fistful of black straws toward the sky. The only sound the crowd ever made was a low repeated cadence which began now: guilty, guilty, guilty.

Justina felt herself thrust into the air, then descend down a long way. Somehow she remembered that her child's voice had come from this canyon, and she relaxed and floated downward. She fell, finally, into supportive arms and was so filled with emotion, both from what had transpired above and her child's defense that, finally, she wept.

And this child of hers, this young woman, a maverick herself, comforted her mother as if she were the child, and Justina awoke, sobbing to find her pillow soaked with perspiration and tears. "Pomp and Circumstance" was playing softly over the FM station on the radio on her night stand.

CHAPTER TWELVE

"Thank God, no roses," she thought as he approached with a bunch of yellow daffodils in his hand. She would have gone over the edge if there were any more roses.

He had the tentative, willing-to-be-lost-and-found look that was so typical of him as well as of all passengers deplaning, looking for someone to recognize and rescue them in this foreign place—the airport— all the same, but different enough to make even a seasoned traveler feel homeless.

Simon, Justina's best friend, was returning from a convention at which he was the keynote speaker; his topic? "Making Marriage Work in the Nineties." Before she had a chance to ask how his presentation had gone, there was the requisite hug and kiss as they met, the daffodils still in his hand.

He offered them to her. "Here, I always think of you as a sunny, yellow field. When I saw these in O'Hare I thought about you. Then I felt really silly bringing them on the plane with me, but there you are... One of the stewardesses put them in water somewhere so they'd stay fresh."

Remembering his discomfiture, he was shy suddenly. "So, a token of my love for you."

When Simon and Justina spoke of their love for each other, it was the love of old friends—they had been friends now for more than fifteen years. Simon was what Justina thought of as a nurturing male—a special breed; chameleonic in his desire to aid the needy but only on his terms; quick to withdraw if anyone demanded more than he chose to offer. Perhaps for Simon, it was his professional training that led him to establish limits.

He was a psychologist. How much more nurturing can one be? For her, he was at times her mentor and her brother and at times her father confessor, a role he had recently adopted after she began her liaison with Sasha.

They had met while working on a college success program for unprepared students, and Simon had developed an inventory for forecasting academic success which had proven successful for him, so he had some limited but nonetheless national exposure now as the author. Too, he had gone back for additional training to become a marriage counselor.

When she had scoffed at his credentials for this new area, he told her that he was better able to maintain objectivity by not bringing any marital baggage of his own with him, but then she reminded him of the Roman Catholic celibate priests.

"But Justina you know I am not celibate..."

"Doesn't make any difference," she shot back. "What can you possibly know about marriage? It's not just sex—although that complicates it mightily. My mother used to shuffle back and forth between skepticism and cynicism about the priests. Depending on her attitude of the week, her question, 'What do they know?' was offered either with a barb or as a true question."

"Yes, well, I can see that you came out of those loins," but it was said kindly.

Justina was the sophisticate; Simon, the Mid-western "farmer's son," as he liked to describe himself. So they gave credence to the aphorism about opposites attracting. Justina loved everything visual; Simon loved invisibility. He would almost sidle into a room taking his bearings, checking everyone out before he made himself known.

They were affectionate, respectful, intimate, but asexual with each other. Simon knew himself well enough to know he could not, would not be capable of making a commitment to any woman—had no desire to. Not that he was a womanizer, but he was also not celibate. And so Justina knew of his liaisons and often wondered how women found him sexually attractive. His friendship with Justina was probably as close as he could get to making a commitment, and the strangeness of their friendship was the subject of much gossip. Mostly—"What does she see in him?"—the implication that they had been having this long-time affair.

Justina was aware of this and secretly liked it... the innuendoes, the pointed references from her female friends. Simon dismissed it when they talked about it. It made him uncomfortable. So she teased him, "Gives you some status you wouldn't otherwise have, doesn't it, having everyone think you're in bed with Mother Superior?"

"So you know what they call you?" Simon was surprised.

"Oh yes. It's something gossips would love to report," and she shrugged her shoulder jauntily. "Which makes it more delicious, don't you see? The joke's on them." And she laughed. Simon hadn't gotten the joke.

Now Justina listened to the scuttlebutt from the convention and the reaction to Simon's presentation as they walked through the airport. They waited at the baggage carousel, still chattering. "So, you've fixed it for all us poor souls out there struggling to make marriage work? Simon to the rescue once again." But this was playful, and she put her hand on his shoulder. "I'm happy for you, even if I am becoming a cynic."

Simon shifted slightly at this public display of affection. "But you're all glowy and breathless in spite of your growing cynicism, so I have to guess you have just seen Sasha or are about to?"

"Two nights ago...." And she avoided his direct glance by sticking her nose into the bouquet.

"Doesn't Wil see that something's going on with you?" And at the shake of her head in denial, he continued, "How are you going to explain when he does?"

They were standing off to the side away from the bodies lining the carousel, and Justina had a fleeting memory of the crowds in her dream. She was thoughtful for a moment. "I don't know. I'm not even sure I'll have to." She made a scowling, sad face. "Maybe it will all be over before he notices."

Simon raised his eyebrows.

"Oh, Simon I don't know; I just don't know. My rational self says this cannot go on at this pace, that it will burn itself out and then no one will ever know that I escaped this world for a few short months." She felt ready to cry at that thought and looked away, for she couldn't cry in front of Simon. That was the one unforgivable sin, and certainly not in a public place.

Simon saw it and gave her the time to gather her emotions together. He knew she would. He had seen her in enough tough situations on the street in the ghettos, in the humblest of dwellings on the Indian reservations where they had worked together to know she could put on her surroundings like a cloak and make them hers. He had never seen anyone uncomfortable with her. "For that matter," he thought, "I've never seen her uncomfortable with any one else."

When he told her, she said quietly, "Thank you, Simon, that's one of the nicest things any one has ever told me about myself. That you would notice, and that you would tell me endears you to me even more." But for now, he could see her becoming once again the traveler, waiting patiently on the fringes of the carousel.

Hours before, she had been feeling incredibly light-headed and giddy when it was time to leave for the airport to meet Simon. And on an impulse, she had called the limo service to hire an ostentatious stretch limousine. It was invisibly tethered in the choicest parking spot right outside.

Justina loved Simon's Mid-west values, not that they were that much different from her own, but he was honest about his which included careful decisions and thrift. He avoided being conspicuous, and conspicuous consumption was an awful violation, the Dr. in front of his name or the Ph.D. behind it notwithstanding. Justina, on the other hand would gladly have died before giving evidence that she wasn't comfortable in any situation. And she enjoyed what money bought. Although she was rarely profligate, she could be very impulsive. Witness the limo.

So they emerged from the airport, and the driver nodded, opened the door, for her and took Simon's bag all in one easy gesture. What could he do but follow? Once inside, she giggled.

"What?" he asked.

"I just had a most delicious thought. I think I'll hire one of these the next time I meet Sasha."

"And pick him up outside the guard's station at the factory? I'm sure that would be a treat."

"Simon, it's not like you to be nasty."

"Was that nasty?" all innocence. Then, "I'm just afraid of so much unbridled happiness, I guess. You know me. And the reality is that I will still be here when he is gone. As your friend, I will have to endure your pain with you. And as your ersatz therapist, I will help you put yourself back together, but it will all be painful for me, too."

"So you don't think it's possible to lead this dual life until it dies a natural death—to have it all for a while and recognize the moment it's over?"

"Darling Tina, it's what I most want for you. Damn it, it's what I and everyone else wants—all my clients. It ALL. But you are vibrating with it. Will it be over for you and Sasha at the same time? That's the question, isn't it?"

They had maneuvered out of the airport complex and were heading back to town.

"Simon, Simon. I know this euphoria will not last. Give me credit. The whole thing is like temporary insanity, and the operative word is temporary. And I want to savor it—every moment of it for as long as it lasts."

"Look, Justina." He had slipped into formality. She knew she was going to be counseled. "Be reasonable. How long has he been in this country? You are probably his dream of what every American woman is all about: You're beautiful on the inside and you look beautiful, classy on the outside, and forgive me, but you don't look your age. You may not be wealthy, but you can afford this on a whim." And Simon waved at the interior of the car. "He's still a boy by our standards."

"Please don't scold me. I know you're being realistic and I'm going to say what every other woman would say. But it's not like that at all. Sasha is still trying to come to grips with his own life in this country, I know. He's still torn. Life is not good in Croatia now, and he still has family there. And he's got family here. I can see the possibility of either of us turning cranky and irritable, this deceit an added burden when we're both reaching overload as it is. And forgive me, but someone growing up in Croatia is not the same as a thirty-year-old American. But for right now, this is the reward we're both getting for putting up with all the rest. So please don't scold me." She looked pleadingly at him. "It's like being surrounded by a wonderful, scented bubble, and I don't want to prick it right now."

"Um. I know. And I don't mean to scold."

And he leaned across the seat and kissed her lightly on the cheek in apology and knocked her hat off. They both laughed and relaxed as she put it back on.

They had come to the Grande Hotel for an early afternoon drink and so Justina could pick up her car which was parked here. It was quiet in the bar in mid afternoon and they took a table in the corner of one of those mahogany-paneled rooms, done in the style of an English gentlemen's club. And the sweet, young woman who came for their orders was dressed in the classic English maid's uniform. Justina almost expected her to curtsy and say, "Yes, Sir. Yes, Mum."

"So, Simon, back to our conversation. Is it possible or even desirable to have it all?" she asked thoughtfully while spreading Stilton cheese on the crackers that had been set before them.

Simon was thoughtful and sipped at his vodka martini. "Some people make accommodations so it seems they have it all…"

Justina interrupted, "Making accommodations is exactly what I've been doing all my life. That's exactly what having it all is NOT about."

"It's an imperfect world, Teenie," his hand, gentle on her knee.

"So do we have to accept what's imperfect or can we…," she stopped in mid sentence, a cracker halfway to her mouth.

"Look, I know this is childish, but I'm American enough to believe that any one can do anything, be anything, work for anything they really want to and achieve it. But that's the myth of the Constitution, isn't it? all of it. But how to let go of such dreams… And then there's your wonderful solution—behavior modification. And we get what we want often enough to keep us on the treadmill." And she popped the cracker into her mouth.

Simon laughed. "You're going to defame the Constitution and behavior modification in one breath? That's why you're such a treat, Justina. I have to be honest with you, I never thought about the Constitution encouraging anyone to have an extra-marital affair." He smiled, and she knew she had been blowing smoke like Puff the Magic Dragon. "But I see what you mean—the endless possibilities. Isn't that a tremendous burden?"

"Of course it is, dammit. I can never be good enough, do enough, have enough. No, that's not true—I'm not acquisitive except for knowledge. But you do see how circular that is? I just need to know more to be better, do better, so I can know more… Oh, shit." And Justina realized she was engaging in one of her major faults, getting preachy. Mostly she was able to forestall it, and now she had a chance to change the subject when the waitress approached to refresh their drinks.

Abruptly switching topics, she said. "Tell me about the new deal."

"Okay, there's a small, but well financed group forming in New York. The tentative plan is to research the effects of women returning to school on marriage and family life." Justina looked askance. "It's still in the primitive stages, but you know and I know how many of my clients and your students go through marital distress during this adjustment. So I'm going to consult with them, mostly long distance, to put the project together. You know, see what if anything has been done already—I can't think of anything off-hand, can you?"

Justina shook her head. "But, I could be your first interviewee…"

"That wasn't what I had in mind for you. No promises, but there may be a place for you. Whaddya think?"

"What kind of place? When? New York?" Sasha was temporarily forgotten. Justina could feel elation growing in her, consuming her.

"It's still in the planning stages, Justina. I just wanted to know if you'd even consider taking a break for a year or two if this all pans out…"

Then her practical side emerged. "But I'd lose all my clients here. I guess I could always come back to the university, and start over…"

"With a very nice addition to your resume, I might add. Look, this is all very iffy at this point, but since the money seems to be there, my guess is it's going to see the light of day. But you know how money can be promised and withdrawn, so don't turn any clients away yet."

Justina was silent, thoughts catapulting over each other— leaving Sasha, her business which was taking off, her comfort at the university—for all her complaints—and finally, Wil.

She drained her wine glass and smiled vaguely. "Well, we'll just have to see, won't we?"

They left in Justina's car. She was to drop Simon off and meet her six o'clock class.

It was when she was finally alone in her car that she thought of that apartment high up on the twenty-second floor of a New York skyscraper.

CHAPTER THIRTEEN

Graduation for most of those in academe—students, faculty, and administration—is Christmas, Thanksgiving, the first day of Spring, and a wedding all rolled into one: ceremony, tradition, celebration, costumes, music. Christmas, because it is the time when the gifts students received are finally made public—their own intellect and curiosity, their dedication. Thanksgiving, because the students are thankful that they made it, and faculty give thanks that some of them squeaked through. The first day of Spring, because it is a time of renewal—yesterday I did not have a degree—that lusted for piece of paper—and today I do. I can add it to my resume, shove it across the desk to prove who I am. And finally, it is the bride and groom of dreams and accomplishment—a moment in time when all believe they will "live happily ever after," make more money, feel more confident in the world.

Justina couldn't help herself. She was always transported seeing "her" students graduate. It was a day of magic. She hadn't felt that way about her own graduations. This was entirely different. She had encouraged and prodded, shown disappointment when in fact she was disappointed, but always she urged her students on, "You know what you have to do? Go do it—and do it well."

But this graduation was more… Sasha was graduating!

Sasha was not only graduating but was to receive the first annual Paul Bowers Award for Excellence. She had been asked to say a few words on his behalf, as his professor, when the award was announced and demurred.

Kate was adamant. "Listen, Tina, you have to. Phelps—you

do remember him? Our president? Your president?—will carry on about the university, and Paul Bowers will carry on about himself, and you'll be able to bring it back to Alexander." The note of sarcasm about remembering Phelps Morrison was not lost on Justina.

Justina was glad everyone referred to him as Alexander. Somehow it made it seem like someone else—not Sasha. But she could not even imagine a worse position to be in: She and Sasha, the two of them together—side by side— standing there on a stage in front of hundreds of students and their families. She knew everyone would see it—this chemistry or electricity between them that didn't need to be verbalized for others to recognize it, feel it. She had witnessed it herself too many times: the realization of the sexual tension between colleagues—too casual? trying too hard to seem unaffected? They couldn't pull it off for someone watching carefully or even for those not watching carefully. Perhaps it was primal—knowing who belonged to whom at a given moment…

"Look, Kate"—they were in Kate's office again—"This is Alexander's moment of glory. Trotting me out there will make it seem as if I had something to do with his success, when you and I both know, it is his moment, his achievement. I didn't do anything different for him from what, I hope, I always do for all my students." And silently she added, At least not for his project. "It was his idea, his identification of the problem, his plan of action, his research. To drag me out there to congratulate him will diminish his own personal accomplishment. And I won't do that."

"Tina, you have been very weird about this whole thing—not taking your place on the selection committee—and now this." Kate was genuinely troubled. "It's not like you. What's going on?"

"Kate, absolutely nothing." She shifted invisibly in her seat. "I told you why I was uncomfortable sitting on that committee which, incidentally, managed quite well without me. And wouldn't it be just ducky now, for me to have sat on that committee with my student winning the prize?" She scoffed. "Please stop reading anything into this. I just feel as if Phelps and Paul are enough. Let's not engage in overkill. There are enough things going on during the ceremony so we don't need to fill up quiet moments—extend the program. You know as well as I do that the students are impatient about all the speakers, all the folderol. They want to hear their names called and have Phelps hand them that phony piece of paper that looks like a degree, shake their hand, congratulate them, wave and blow kisses to the audience, and prance off stage—degreed!

She leaned forward—a warmer, friendlier gesture—then quizzically, "Did you ever notice their demeanor—their formal march up to Phelps—and the next moment, as if they've finally, really been let out of school, even the most decorous of them, walking off with hurried steps—almost as if they're afraid Phelps will turn and call them back—tell them it was all a mistake?"

Her hands rose from her lap, separated, palms up—an offering. "Anyway, Paul Bowers, bless him, is looking for his own moment in the sun. Give it to him. He'll probably carry on ad infinitum about dear old Drysdale U and his student days here and bore the current crop to tears. So my answer is, 'No'." And Justina looked Kate directly in the eye.

Kate looked thoughtfully across her desk at Justina. "Well, obviously I can't compel you to do this… At least you'll be there, won't you?"

Justina snorted. "How long have I been here? ten years? twelve? Have I ever missed graduation? Of course I'll be there. Do you need a hand with anything?" When Kate shook her head, Justina said, "Well, I just thought I'd ask so you don't think I'm being recalcitrant."

"Recalcitrant? No, I don't think that. It's just that I could always count on you for anything, and now you're somehow different— more removed. I don't know…" And Kate lowered her gaze, so as not to offend her with a more challenging glance.

Justina felt a genuine pang—guilt, she knew—for dissembling with Kate. They were faculty together in their early days, before Kate decided she wanted to get out of the classroom. "Kate, remember the conversation we had that other time we visited this issue? I'm busier now than I used to be—going in multiple directions. I don't mean to be 'removed' as you call it; I really am just busier."

"And," she thought, "I still have to leave time for Sasha, but this is not one of those times."

She headed for the door, then paused. "Look, after graduation, let's take an afternoon off. We'll have lunch and a couple glasses of wine and catch up." And then as an added sop, because Justina disliked shopping and especially disliked shopping with anyone else, "We can shop…"

"But you hate to shop…"

"See? That's how much I'm trying to set things right." And Justina turned at the doorway, "See ya' before that—at graduation."

CHAPTER FOURTEEN

Shiny, ebony wood appointments contrasted sharply with the pale, rose suede interior of the white limousine. It had the elegance of a New York art deco apartment of the thirties or perhaps a yacht. Justina said, "Yes, this one," when she was being shown the limousines available for the night she and Sasha had agreed to meet.

Her plan was that they would meet under the porte cochere of the Regency at exactly six o'clock. She had arranged everything down to the last detail: The car would slide alongside, the driver would open the limousine door for him, and they would be spirited away for a few hours of pleasure.

She wore only three pieces of clothing under the full length black mink coat: a full-skirted quiet black silk dress with a V-neck created by crossing two separate pieces of fabric caught at the waist, around which was a pale rose velvet cummerbund; one of those pink lace bras which were new to her wardrobe; and a pair of black pantyhose with the crotch cut out. She mentally thanked a colleague from whom she had learned some time ago that panty hose wouldn't run if you cut on the inside of the crotch seam.

She wore creamy white pearls which hung just to the neckline of her dress. She had learned early on that Sasha loved the play involved in figuring out jewelry clasps, each one of them different. Bra hooks were pretty basic. The only thing that changed was the number of them or a front clasp, and she had some of those in her stash, too.

Most of the fun of this was in the contrast and the dare-devilness of it. Sasha would be in his jeans with one of the open necked silk shirts he was fond of. And while this night would not fit his definition of spontaneous (since it had taken such careful planning), it would have the element of surprise. And contrast. And some risk of discovery. There was the driver, after all.

There was wine in a cooler and in her basket his favorite Polish sausage and her favorite Stilton cheese and crackers. Bach's Brandenburg concertos played softly in the background. She hadn't timed them, only now as they were approaching the hotel, wondering if they would last...

He was there! The car slid to a stop. Sasha looked casually the other way. The driver got out, opened the door and motioned him in.

He paled at the shock. This he had not expected. Justina held her breath. But he was up to it. He recovered quickly.

He slid into the car, then slid his hand under her dress and coat and up the outside of her thigh and kissed her longingly, sweetly, gently, demandingly. Ecstasy. He whispered something in Croatian in her ear and it sounded lovely. She knew if she could translate those words properly, they would become fact. Later...

"Wine, my Love?" she asked.

He settled back, prepared to enjoy himself, and examined their environment. "I can't top this," he said, exhaling.

"It's not a contest, my darling. And you could top this easily with a picnic in your truck. The environment is merely the icing—we're what's happening and that's all that counts."

A crumb from a cracker fell on her bosom. Sasha picked it off from the fur and opened her coat. "Are you really hungry?" he asked.

"Ummm," she replied. "But not necessarily for the cheese and crackers."

She had checked out the privacy issue. Enough. The music would help.

For Sasha's finger was now following the shape of her lips, and then parting her lips, forcing her to take that finger into her mouth. Promises, wild and wonderful promises. His other hand caressed the back of her neck, fingers gently finding their way under the neckline of her dress. He moved her from side to side to take her coat off and eventually it fell to the floor. He kissed the hollow of her neck, separated the two folds of fabric and looked down appreciatively at the pink lace bra. Cupping her breasts in his hands outside of her dress, he buried his head in them.

Justina ran her hands through his hair; his hair looked coarse and was curly but was so incredibly soft it was always a surprise to her. She buried her nose in his hair, inhaling his scent.

"Wonderful, exciting, lovely bitch," he whispered.

"What did you say before in Croatian?" she asked.

Early on, when she didn't know if their telephone calls were being monitored, she would ask him to say lovely things to her in Croatian. Later when they met, she got to "translate" what it was he had said. If she guessed correctly, they got to do it. She was at his mercy, and in this, she knew he was not to be trusted. She was very imaginative, and he almost always assured her that her translation was accurate. She was never disappointed although her expertise with the Croatian language was exactly nil.

"What do you think I said?" he asked softly in her ear.

"Well, let's see." She paused for a long, time, teasing. "I think it was that you'd like to make love on a black mink blanket in the back of a white limousine with all our clothes on."

"You're doing so well with the language, Dear One. I must be a good teacher. You were close. But I didn't say anything about leaving all our clothes on. A bit difficult to manage, I think. No?"

"Well, I'm sure that's what you said, but I stand corrected. I think we can manage anyway. Let's make the rules: You may have anything you want but only my pearls can be taken off and nothing can be pulled down. Same for me."

Suddenly he tenderly thrust his hand up her skirt. "Bingo!" He was now into the game.

She unbuttoned his jeans. "No," he said. "You said nothing could be taken off or pulled down."

"But I'm not, uh, taking anything off or pulling anything down yet."

"How will you get him out then?"

She reached into her purse, brought out a small pair of manicuring scissors and cut his bikini undershorts so they fell away in the front, still staying within the rules.

His penis, with the red rosebud tip was free. "I brought you another pair, so you can go home the way you left this morning. I know you always wear white…"

There is this about Bach: He wrote enough Brandenburg Concertos. Or else they didn't notice that they were repeating.

CHAPTER FIFTEEN

Several months had passed since Simon had first told Justina about the project he was involved with in New York. He had made two or three trips back there for face-to-face meetings, and Justina knew the time was drawing near when he would know whether it was go or no-go.

Over those several months, the focus of the project (and the money men) had changed considerably. So many national companies were offering full or partial tuition reimbursements to their employees to encourage them to continue their education. The fallout was that many of these employees were going through divorces, working, and going to school. So now the question was more focused, and they would be using these employee/students for their studies.

Did they think the companies had a conscience? They did not. It was all cost benefits. Many of the employees were valuable assets to their companies, and dissatisfaction, whatever the source, was to be eliminated or at least reduced. The companies all wanted a happy work force since a happy work force increased production, especially when everyone had to do more with less. It all seemed a bit ludicrous to Simon and Justina with all the down-sizing and right-sizing going on, but if someone wanted to pay them mega bucks to investigate, they were their team. There was the other component to their research: Marital counseling was to be offered as another benefit.

When the bouquet of yellow roses was delivered, Justina was not surprised when she opened the envelope that came with them. "Pack your bags. You're going to New York! We're in!"

Justina called Simon to thank him for the flowers. "Well, daffodils just didn't seem important enough to mark the start of something this big," he said. But of course, from Simon, they had to be yellow.

After much soul-searching and examining their schedules for the next few months, they decided that Justina would go to New York to get the administrative phases under way. So she could go to "The City" and live out her dream without inflicting pain. Simon would stay for a few more months and close down his practice for now and commute whenever possible and/or necessary.

Justina was in the middle of two classes and had many more scheduled, but with six weeks to spare before any new classes began, the university could find replacements. After ten years as adjunct faculty and department chair, it seems she was easy to replace.

Adjunct faculty have a special place in the university hierarchy. The university could not operate without them, but unlike corporations who want to keep their employees happy at all costs, universities offer no benefits to these employees no matter how long they've taught. Problems? "Why don't you take a sabbatical?" Without pay, of course.

In her early days in the state system, when faculty were asking for more money, one of the college presidents (in private, naturally) dismissed their request with the comment, "There are at least four more of them standing on each corner of every major intersection in the city." Quite a different attitude in the academic environment from the one Justina was about to enter.

Justina always had Wil's support, whether while working on her Ph.D., while pregnant or working in general—even the crazy night classes as adjunct faculty. And so he still supported her and even encouraged her in this, too. There would be enough money so he could jet to the city for weekends, and they worked out tentative schedules. Both still had family on the East coast, so it became an exciting chance to renew old acquaintances and reunite with family. They laughed at looking forward to that. One of the reasons they had moved west was to get away from family.

All her other projects were portable or could be picked up by a colleague. Her business, J. L. Packard and Associates, had been called that in anticipation of needing "associates," and now she did. And she called on them, and they were eager for the additional work themselves.

She was ecstatic on the one hand, sorrowing on the other. She would get to live in "The City"—the city she had never lived in, although she had briefly worked there. In the fifties, when one married, one moved out of the city to the suburbs where she had always lived. Yet the longing to be a "New Yorker" was with her still.

But there was Sasha.

She knew if he had the opportunity to go to a new city (and there was some discussion about this), he would go. They had already talked about his chances for even further advancement since his promotion before graduation and then his winning the Paul Bowers Award. And Justina accepted it. Being ready for him to leave was a constant in her relationship with him. But until recently, she had never considered that she would be the one to go.

She called him rarely, although she wanted to call him constantly, even now, almost a year since that night in the car. He knew about the project she and Simon were working on and he was happy for her. But he got that information as a result of his calls to her, and the infrequent times they discussed it when they were together. Now she had to tell him that she was leaving sort of permanently to live in New York.

So she made the early morning call from bed.

Sasha was—well, Sasha. He expressed pleasure because he knew how much she wanted to return to the city. But she wanted his sorrow, his agony. She wanted him to plead with her not to go. She wanted him to beg her to stay, to be there with him. She wanted tantrums and tears, wild threats. She understood that she would have gone anyway, but she wanted to know she would be leaving him with an empty, black hole in his life that no one else could fill—that she was irreplaceable—that he would die a certain death without her. She knew none of this was true. But she wanted him to say it anyway. And… she wanted it to be true.

If he knew that about Justina, he gave no evidence of it. She knew he was incapable of such ravings. Perhaps once—for Nadja—but he had insulated himself against caring so much ever again. He had his work.

So they had a sensible conversation about the details of her going—when she would leave, whether the project muckity-mucks would find an apartment for her, how often she'd get back to town, and even whether there was a chance he'd get to New York on business of his own. They were sane, stable—neither of them saying the wrong thing—or the right thing.

Finally, a hesitant, "Justina, I will miss you. We will not have our long telephone conversations. Even the times we were able to make together…"

"Yes, I know. I want to scream for more time, pound on the chest of the gods who have not fixed it better for us. Long nights with no leavings, no going back to some other beds. Oh, Sasha, some part of me will surely die without you. You gave me back to myself in ways you will never know."

"Sweet one, you will be back in town. With how often we seem to be able to arrange our times together, it won't be much different…"

"It will be different! We will be 2,000 miles away from each other. I always think about the chances: If you can get away… if I have time. With ten miles between us, there is always the possibility. If I have time and I am in New York and you are here, even if you could get away, what good is it?"

"Justina, we knew—we knew when we started this that it was not going to be easy. This is just one more fold."

"Fold? Fold? Oh, you mean wrinkle, dammit. Wrinkle. No… You're right. It is a fold. A fold is more closed, more final than a wrinkle. I'd like it to be a wrinkle if it has to be, but you're right. It's a fold. Ironed shut, pressed along the edge, closed."

"But we've had so much, Justina. It isn't as if it's over. We're still the same people we were last week, yesterday, the weekend in the glass house."

"No, we aren't. I knew yesterday I was going. I just couldn't call you then."

"But you know what I mean. You are always making me stay with the argument at hand, and now you're changing it. Nothing that has happened can change. We have had wonderful moments together, more than most people ever have. No one, not even time can take those away. You will take those with you to New York, and you'll be a sensation there just as you are here. My life will go on, and instead of wondering what we might have been like together, I know. I can replay those scenes whenever I need to, to keep me going. You will always be with me in that way."

"But I'm not a sensation here. That's just your view of me. I am plodding, trying to find myself, be honest with myself and the world and I'm not even doing a good job of that."

"You're moving our discussion sideways again. Come on. You know you have influenced lots of people positively at the university. Look what you've done for me! Most people would be pretty satisfied with the successes you've had, the influence…"

"If I were most people, you would never have even been interested in me. It's because I'm not most people that you were attracted."

"Of course, so what more do you want from yourself and from me?"

"Sasha, Sasha, I want everything! The music, the pleasure, knowledge, you, the smells, the feel, the agony and the exquisite sense of being alive—you, passion, not just sexual passion, but passion for life. And I don't want it to end or be diminished."

"Greedy child; you're like that in bed, too. Don't you know you've had more than most people because you've wanted more than most people even dream about? Justina, you're a dreamer, but you're also a doer. Remember that afternoon on the sacred mountain?"

"We've never been together on the sacred mountain. What do you mean?"

"Oh, that's right. It was a very real dream I had. I'll tell you about it someday. But you were flying around in the sky, and the last words you said to me before you took off for good, were, 'We are all alone—that's what freedom is.' And I understood it so well then. You can't exchange what you think is the prison of your marriage for the bondage of your love for me. You're looking for freedom, but you're not free if you need me this much. Don't you see that?"

"But prisons are only for what you don't want. If you choose to be where you are, it is not a prison. It's only a prison when you're there against your will, or when you want to leave, you do not go—out of guilt or whatever. But it's still against your will. Do you see what I mean?"

And in that moment before Sasha responded, she thought of her guilt— as elusive as a bird in flight. She would catch it if she could, pin it down and look at it critically. But no! It is off on wings, and she thought in a moment of enlightenment, just as well—if I could hold it in my hand I would feel the flutter of its little heart, know it lives, and that knowledge is as harrowing as death, for guilt is a kind of death of the spirit.

Sasha broke into her thoughts, gently. "It's still not any better for you to need me so much than it is for you to be married—which you resist so much right now—if what you want is freedom."

She was quiet, absorbing his words which struck a chord with her.

"So what you're telling me is I have exchanged one prison for another, perhaps more attractive one?"

"Yes. But they are both pleasant prisons for you, and what you want most, I think, is to shake the bars and rebel against them. You would hate a man who was constantly after you—you'd get rid of him in a minute. One of the reasons you're so absorbed with me is because I am not totally available, not entirely at your beck and call—is that the right words? I'm not discounting your real feelings. I've even grown to know they're sincere, but I am not even important enough in your total life to influence you this much. You make more out of me than I am because you need me to be that person."

She was angry. This was not the way she wanted to leave town— angry at Sasha. "I'll have to think about it. It'll become another flag burning we can argue into your old age." And she changed the subject. "I have about six weeks. Will I see you before I leave?"

"Dearest, you're angry. Don't be. It doesn't change anything. We are both who we are. I am that patient donkey, standing there watching you spread you wings and scatter fairy dust down on the rest of us. I'm just happy to catch some of it. Justina, listen, have you ever seen a donkey covered with gold dust? That's how you make me feel, both ridiculous and glamorous."

She said nothing, and into her silence, Sasha quietly said, "Aren't we both better for having been together? I know I am."

She knew better than to continue the conversation because she was overcome. She wanted to cry.

How could she argue? Sasha had the wisdom of centuries behind him, with his centuries old eyes and centuries of weariness which she had not been able to lift or dispel.

Am I a lightweight parading as an intellectual? What do I know and what do I need to know about myself, about freedom? What was it Sasha had said—that I said, "We are all alone—that's what freedom is." Is it possible to be free or even to desire freedom if it means being alone?

She sighed and continued her mental beating. But when all is said and done, we are alone. We have only who we are, what we're capable of doing, who we can become. Am I making more out of this search for freedom, or should I have already known? Or is it all just one more journey which I am dramatizing? Does everyone shed one burden only to replace it with another? Am I even capable of enjoying real freedom, or would I forever carry the baggage of past and present lives with me? Does everyone? Is there nothing unique about my search? Do my passions imprison me in ways I have not yet even suspected?

Justina turned into her pillow; she would have to think about it all in New York…

She left six weeks later.

She and Sasha had one grand evening. It was the same and it was different. It was hello and goodbye—new and final—as all of their couplings were. It was never lost on Justina that every moment they spent together might be the last. Who knew what happened between times? Overwhelming guilt? Certainly for her, it was always possible that she would be overcome and unable to continue. Exposure? That would surely toll the knell of death for their relationship. Change of jobs? Sasha was moving up and the potential for him to move on was always present. But neither of them had given much thought to the fact that she would be the one to go.

And now they were face to face with her leaving...

They loved each other that night as if they did not already know each other: fiercely—memorizing the secret folds and creases and curves of their bodies; gently—fairy wings barely whispering on their skins to strike chords that resonated in other secret places within; seductively—teasing, pleasuring, dancing a horizontal tango; hungrily—for they had not yet dined fully on this feast; yet patiently. It would be over much too soon.

They breathed as one, inhaling and exhaling in concert. She felt his heart beat against hers. She felt his warm semen swimming within her even after he was no longer there. She heard the dinging of his watch each hour as she always did, silently, painfully, on some level counting how much time was left before they had to separate. They knew nothing would ever be the same again. The next time, if there would even be a next time, they would each be quite different people as they danced to the slow waltz time and space performed. And his watch dinged their last hour...

She thought about it on the way home, and realized that every time they were together, they were subtly different people from whom they had been before. Even their loving changed—and changed them from one time to the next. And Sasha was right about this at least. "Not about the flag burning," she thought, "But we had what we created and nothing, no one, could change that even though our time together has changed us."

She had written a poem to Sasha and had it translated into Greek by a Greek student currently in her class. She sealed it first in a passionate purple envelope, then inserted it into a plain white envelope and gave it to the florist to deliver to him at his office the morning after she left with a single red rose.

Smile…
Eroded, excised, extinguished, exfoliated by
Waves…
Flash, smash, splash and dash to the sea with my
Tears…
Soft, sorrowing, sinuous salt on my cheek—
Brine…
From the eternal sea of my love for you.
Heart…
Fragile, frail, fretful, frantic, frenetic
Without you…

Simon was at the airport when Wil and Justina arrived. As the three of them strode through the airport, she saw Sasha, standing off to the side, and she remembered the night at the concert. Here he was again in his black leather coat, leaning against the far wall, watching, smiling sadly. She could smell his smell, smell the leather of his coat. And once again, she was dragged mentally into that force field he created. She missed a step.

He was holding a single red rose with which he silently saluted her as their eyes met. It was a gesture unnoticed by others. Over the airport PA system, Frank Sinatra was singing, "New York, New York;" but Justina was listening to the Rachmaninov piano concerto.

"Dear Sasha," she thought, "You taught me more than I ever taught you."

SASHA

What is life? It is the flash of a
firefly in the night. It is the breath
of a buffalo in the winter-time. It
is the little shadow which runs
across the grass and loses itself
in the sunset.

Crowfoot (1821-1890)
Blackfoot Confederacy

CHAPTER ONE

I had just come out of one of those meetings where everyone was blaming everyone else for having lost a $3 million deal. I hated this part of this job and sometimes I wished I were back in the plant where things were more concrete. I knew the guy who would ultimately have to accept the blame was not really the one who was at fault. Just another fall guy necessary to protect the jokers around here. I didn't really like him, but that didn't mean I didn't feel for him. I could imagine how he felt, and how I would feel in his place. And I was depressed.

The phone was ringing as I got back to my office. I had half a moment when I thought, "Oh, fuck it," and wasn't going to answer it. But then I thought it would take more time later to return the call and probably play telephone tag with whoever it was, so I answered it. It was Justina.

She rarely called me. She said at the beginning that it was important for me to keep control of our relationship, and that was one way I could do it—by not having her intrude. (Besides she really never believed my phone wasn't tapped—whatever difference that made in who called whom.) I was always pleased when I heard her voice, knowing she would lighten my day, make me laugh. And I needed some of her irreverence now to put this whole thing in perspective.

But it was not my lucky day.

I was already worn down by the day's events, and now she was calling to tell me she was moving to New York, semi permanently, whatever the hell that meant. I still had to store such strange pairing of words that she used and try to translate them later. But I knew the essence of her message. She was, now, in fact, flying away once again as she had done on the mountaintop in my dream.

Actually, it was good that she called now, when I could not gather the emotion to think clearly about what all this would mean to me. So I disappointed her. How could I tell her over the telephone, that strange instrument which tied us together but provided no physical contact that I was already living in a darkened world where her light, almost the only light I had, would now be extinguished?

We had an unsatisfactory conversation; she needed my emotion and I had already spent it in the meeting. So I heard what she was saying, but I couldn't deal with it right then. Actually, I didn't want to deal with it—at all. I had grown to accept that she would always be there; I had learned to use her energy to infuse mine which was constantly ebbing, running out of me, it seemed, as if I had turned on the spigot. I could not switch psychic gears the way she could. When I was stressed as I was then, I could not, just because she called, let go of my mood and buy into hers.

Later, during the six weeks we had before she left, I tried to reach her, to let her know how hollow I felt, the emptiness I looked forward to without her, the panic I could feel building. But I was too late; she had moved into a state of protecting herself and didn't want to speak about it. Suddenly, she didn't want to talk about her going at all, said, "Let's just pretend I'm not leaving and carry on as we were, Sasha." I was alone in my head and my heart trying to analyze our relationship and why I was experiencing such a sense of loss. After all, she was the one who said, and I agreed, "It's just play." So why this trauma and drama?

I recalled the fantasies I had about her and then the reality of her. Early on I was satisfied with the fantasies, never dreaming of anything more. Perhaps those are the best fantasies—those made up out of whole cloth. None of the reality of her existence, her commitments to others, if she even had those, intruded. I was free to pursue her mentally without any of those constraints reality brings and sing my very own song to her. And I could produce them at will.

The reality was far, far better—exquisite, fun, play, excitement, new experiences. When we were together, she could transport me out of myself and take me to other places —places where everything is the way you dream it's going to be when you're young. And even as I think that, I realize I am young by most standards, so why do I feel so old and hardened?

I can't explain it to myself. How could I explain it to her? It was as if the rest of the world just vanished except for that one brilliant spot of light when we were together. I felt spontaneous and open, available. I was real with her, not the person everyone else knew or even how I knew myself—cautious, wary, untrusting. It was as if she found in me, the man, the dreamy, idealistic boy I forgot. And she forced me, somehow, to remember him, to give him birth once again, and now I long for him.

Mostly, I learned to enjoy and treasure everything she had to offer, and I had so much I wanted to give her of this real self which, when I think about it, may not have been enough, but it was everything I had. She could take my pain and make it vanish, even if only temporarily while we were together. It's funny, she could make me angry, too, but not for long.

But when we parted each time, we had to deal with all the other realities: the constant fear that we would be discovered—time, work, the others in our lives, and always the guilt.

Men and women must think and feel differently about what we were doing, because Justina was consumed with guilt. If she could have, she would have put it in her pocket to take out and analyze routinely—like trying to take the seeds out of a strawberry. I tried not to think about it all. I did, but I tried not to.

Justina said guilt in our case was worse than sin. Your sins could be forgiven, but you were still stuck with the knowledge that you had committed the sin. And then she laughed. "You know what? When I was a small girl, going to catechism classes, our nun told us our souls were like the white host we would receive at communion. But when we sinned, we got a black spot on our souls. For years I thought my soul looked like a Dalmatian."

We were in bed alongside each other, and she rose up on her elbow and looked at me. "So do you think we get one black spot for each sin, or one for each time we commit the sin—or do you suppose the first black spot just gets bigger and bigger every time you repeat it, like a drop of ink on a blotter? You know how it drops and then just keeps spreading? Do you suppose I'm going to end up with a totally black soul, Sasha? For loving you?"

She was serious and thoughtful for a moment, "No, I could love you without sinning; it's making love that is the sin." And her mood changed as swiftly as it had appeared, "So since I'm beyond redemption, we might as well enjoy it." And her lips were on mine before I could respond to her question, so I responded to her kiss and the promise of what it foretold.

That was so like Justina and why she fascinated me so. She could be so serious and sincere—philosophical, even—talking about sin and redemption, and then throw it all to the wind and become a temptress—as if such thoughts never troubled her. When I was with her, I could shed my troubles the same way—like those animals that molt—and I always felt as if this time, this new skin would be permanent. And it was—so long as I was with her.

And now she was leaving...

Our last night together had the same ecstasy we always knew together, but the pain I was feeling was one Justina could not make disappear because she was feeling it, too. It was all the more intense because we did not speak of it.

There is a quality to loving that has an iota of pain in it anyway. I've heard that climactic moment described as a little death. I don't know why that is—a moment of fear that this will be the last time? Or do we really lose ourselves in those seconds when we are so joined to another soul that we are truly one? With Justina, I know that exquisite moment when every fiber of my being is called upon and I am euphorically lost in her.

It wasn't just her body I desired, I wanted her essence—all of her. Her ideas, her thoughts, her laughter and fun were as foreign to me as I was foreign to this country. I wanted her freedom to be my freedom—to be able to have a quirky notion flash through my mind and articulate it without caring where it landed when I spoke—there on the table or tossed into the atmosphere gathering momentum and gravitas. Instead, I am this cautious, plodding man who disappears in her presence and becomes—what's the word?—scintillating to her and even to myself.

I went to the airport to watch her go. As I passed the flower seller, I suddenly turned back and bought one red rose. I knew I would not be able to give it to her, but if she saw me, she would remember and know I was remembering and knowing while I waited.

CHAPTER TWO

B ut all that came after…
The first time I saw her I was sitting at one of the long, narrow tables in the company training rooms, feeling a bit half-hearted. With everything else going on in my life—Anna was being a bitch; my granny was demanding and although I loved her more than anyone in the world, she consumed much of my time and attention; the kids were noisy; I despised my job although my current manager was the best one I had had to date—what was I doing enrolling in another class? My last class I had anticipated eagerly; now I wasn't so sure.

My classmates were posturing and I was turned off. We were a strange mixture of company people having come late to pursue a bachelor's degree in management. So we had some upper level people (older) and some of what are frequently referred to as "floor people"—those who did the actual work and were generally younger. I was one of those, a technician, supervising fifteen production workers. In the early classes two small study teams of those higher-level managers formed and stayed together. They had risen to their positions on the basis of seniority and experience and could go no further up the ladder without that "piece of paper." And then there were the rest of us whose study teams changed as one or another of us dropped out temporarily. It was no surprise that our study teams had assembled along the lines of the company hierarchy. I've found little spontaneous democracy in this country.

The worst part of it was that I was eager—eager to learn, eager to grow, eager to reach out to new experiences. What I had learned quickly, however, was that one didn't display such eagerness, at least not in this environment, which was the only one I had at the moment. So I concealed that eagerness publicly and worked quietly, mostly to satisfy my own curiosity, denying credit for much that I did. Along with the inherent differences in my European attitude, for which I was alternately excused and discriminated against, I was probably described by my co-workers as devil-may-care. But that was an attitude I put on like a cloak to keep myself safe. I had also learned to be brutally honest. I'd found that no one quite believed you when you told the truth, particularly if you adopted a cavalier air and even more so, if they didn't really want to believe you. So honesty became my greatest defense—or was it an offense?

Anyway, there we were, all sitting around these rectangular tables bitching and whining, mostly complaining about our grades from the last class, jealousy evident from those who had not fared so well as others, anxious about this class for a variety of reasons.

The door opened and the last of the afternoon sun created a stream of light into which our new prof walked. She wore a tailored, severe blue suit, the color of the Aegean Sea at sunrise. I found it hard to take my next breath, so unexpected was this picture. Not that she was beautiful, but she was certainly female. The light shone upon her in such a way that I thought of those religious pictures— the ones with Heaven's rays pouring down on the saints. I thought I knew how she would smell if I got closer. Her posture erect, she was self-confident, comfortable.

But this was not her environment; I could tell at once. And if we had to have someone who wasn't "one of us," we were hoping for a pushover—someone we could make uncomfortable—a woman we could intimidate and harass a bit instead of the portly, rigid male who had been our last professor, or the dowdy, sag-breasted matron before him, with glasses on the end of her nose wearing a printed polyester dress. This was not that woman!

No one else reacted that I could see. Sometimes I think Americans are totally insensitive, certainly to the subtleties of life, but as in this case, to refined sensuality. Maybe they've seen it all already, and my eyes have not yet grown weary…

There was a pause into which she smiled pleasantly and casually at each of us. She laid the materials she was carrying on the table which had been set aside for her, checked out the overhead projector, and began arranging sets of papers.

She was organized in a totally disorganized kind of way. She made me smile. Within minutes of her arrival, her table was full of "stuff"—stacks of papers, transparencies, books—all kinds of disarray. But she remained cool and in command. "A very attractive woman," I thought, "but one with some kind of difference. We'll see; we'll see," I added silently, reserving any judgment.

She left the training room and soon returned into that path of sunlight carrying a styrofoam cup full of water. Idly, I wondered if she knew how she looked entering and was deliberately using it to create an impression. Yet precisely at four o'clock, she turned professional; introduced herself: Justina Packard; we could call her Tina. I don't remember all of it. I only remember wanting to watch her, to impress her, to have her remember me. I was—what is the word—smitten? She was the embodiment of womanhood to me that day. She is now. She will always be some kind of standard.

Fun then, and the testing and setting up that goes on the first minutes of a new class. I had an opportunity to try to unsettle her as she tried to pronounce my name. "No, that's not quite it. Try the accent on…" But she was not dismayed and seemed to enjoy the exchange. The rest of the class laughed as we went back and forth, and I finally let her off the hook. "Close enough."

She made some attempt to personalize each student's introduction. "Yes, my father was a pipe fitter," she nodded in response to one student's stated occupation. But she had traveled far from the blue-collar environment her father had worked in. That was obvious.

Within a very short time we were united as a class as we never had been before—a group of students working on a Harvard Review case study related to organizational behavior. She moved us around, got us to work with each other, changed where we sat. It is always challenging with these case studies to look at the theories and the concepts—to eliminate preconceived notions and the shabby treatment we sometimes received—and arrive at a creative solution. So we blamed, discussed, gained some insight as she moved deliberately among us, asking questions, making suggestions, offering advice as each group examined the issues and formulated a plan of action.

When she announced it was time for a break, no one could believe it. Usually, we were all glancing at our watches waiting impatiently to be released, even if only for that fifteen-minute break. We walked away in the groups to which she had assigned us—a first—still discussing the case study.

"Boy, I'm glad I didn't miss this one," someone said, and there was unanimous agreement among us as went to the vending machines, used the bathroom.

It was the same when we returned, and it was time to leave before we noticed we had been there for four hours.

It was late September and the night air was clear and chilly, refreshing after working inside all day long and the added four more hours of class. More than twelve hours had passed since I had parked my truck in the parking lot. The day had been pretty much like any other, and I wasn't looking forward to the additional work of this class. She wasn't going to be easy to please, this Tina Packard, but I was surely going to try. Yet, when I climbed into my truck, I felt lighter, hopeful, expectant, and full of anticipation, more like I had years before in Zagreb.

It is hard now to imagine that those days ever were; moreover, that they had been my days and nights—a young life filled with my dreams of America: fast cars, beautiful women, nights filled with sex with Nadja, and finally, lots of money.

Well, I am here. I have a house in the suburbs with the required mortgage; a four-year-old Japanese truck; a wife who doesn't much care about sex; three kids I don't understand, and more money than I ever dreamed I would make. I suppose it is just never enough. Less than a dream, it has the scary quality of a subtle nightmare— elusive, quiet, and dark, and yet, I don't know if I want to wake up yet—or at all.

I feel as if I'm always on "hold" and waiting; waiting to see what will happen next; waiting to see who will respond; waiting to see what part I have to play. It's like elevator music in the background of my life, designed to pacify those of us who must wait, and it speaks not at all to me. I'm cradling a silent phone between my shoulder and my ear.

I can't define my life in a single word—happy is not it—but I don't know how to change it or what that would require. Or even if such change would be better. So with quiet fear and much disillusion, I have come to realize the expectations and enthusiasm I once had have slowly, quietly disappeared as if they were wind I gathered in my fist. I have this vague memory of how they felt, but I no longer experience the sensations…

When I drove home that night, I fantasized about driving right past my neighborhood and going to the lake about ten miles away, but even as I thought about it, I knew I'd have to explain why I was late, where I had been, who I had been with. The anticipated pleasure drowned in reality, like the kittens I'd once had to drown when I was a kid. I choked at the cost and pulled into my own driveway and sat there for a moment.

It's not that I don't care about my family—and Anna, too, I guess. When Nadja left me, I vowed I'd never trust another woman again, and it's hard to love someone you won't let yourself trust. I don't know if I love Anna, if I ever loved her, if I even want to love her. Yet, we've been married for almost eight years. It's a hell of a way to live, and it's not what I wanted or expected, but I made the deal and I'll live with it. Maybe I do love her, or maybe I just don't know what "love" is. At any rate, this is not what I thought it would be.

I do know I don't feel good about living in a country where money is the only thing that seems important because now it's become too important to me. I don't feel good—about my marriage which is more like a European marriage than an American one and yet so much less, about my job, about my kids…

Yet here I was, humming to the last strains of the music on my truck radio. What had changed? Absolutely nothing, Sasha, you donkey. Not a damned thing. But I felt as if I were smiling.

CHAPTER THREE

The weeks went by quickly, strips of ordinary time on a calendar with that one bright spot off center each Thursday. It was crazy, anticipating going to class as much as I did. If someone had asked for the details of what Tina Packard taught, I would have been vague, "Something about organizational behavior."

Yet it was easy for me and the others to translate the concepts into our workplace and see both how ordinary and how bizarre our own organization was. We learned that we were a pretty typical Fortune 500 company, although many of us wondered how that had happened—the Fortune 500 thing—given the kind of operation we witnessed daily.

And then she was gone.

After that first class with Tina, our study teams changed slightly. Some who had hardly spoken with others stayed in those new groups formed that first night of Tina's class. And amazingly, there were no hard feelings. American democracy does work, given the opportunity! I had always been glad that my own manager was not among my classmates. I saw how uncomfortable it could be taking a different point of view from your manager even when it was just a case study, an assignment.

A few months later, unexpectedly, she reappeared as our business research project instructor. The man who was originally assigned to this class had had a mild heart attack and was recovering. I was a few minutes late—a problem on the floor. She was in the classroom before me, and the winter light was different, so there was no way to recreate her first entry. There was no need to; I would never forget the original. She looked up briefly and said, "Okay, now we can begin. Sasha's here." But she said it with a smile and got the group to chuckle. They raised a few eyebrows in my direction, and I played the buffoon a bit.

I thought, "So she remembers me." And here I was again with the same happy, silly, childish feeling upon seeing her.

She was exciting in the classroom. It was pretty obvious she enjoyed being there; it was like a contest for her. Could she move us, even the slow starters away from the starting gate and get us into the race? She loved the challenge, and she loved to challenge us—leading us in one direction, then switching sides and turning suddenly so we knew we had been had. Even her body language telegraphed her intention to make us think—to go beyond the obvious, to be creative, to think "outside the box."

During one class she showed a film about paradigms and how our investment in our own ideas and our expectations hinder us from adopting new ones—even in scientific experiments. It was powerful stuff…

In another class when she was trying to get us to understand the merits of research and looking at all sides of the problem, she stopped suddenly and looked around the room, searching for something. She walked over to the waste basket in the corner and picked it up, holding it in front of her. She took a piece of blank paper, wrote something on it, held it against the back side of the basket and said, "This is a waste basket. Looks very ordinary, right? But let's say this is an idea, any idea. Well, what did I just write on this side? You can't see?"

We stared in silence. Obviously, we had no idea. She let the silence last, and then finally, turned the basket around. "You can't contemplate an idea or a problem unless you look at it from all sides." On the sheet of paper, she had written, "Save."

"It's difficult to associate a waste basket with save, isn't it, if all you're thinking about is the waste basket and throw-aways. But think of all the connections between waste and save," and she paused as we did just that. "If you don't turn your ideas around, turn them inside out, look at the backside and the underbellies, you will have failed in researching a problem."

"Now how much time do you have for your particular problems? Not enough. There is never enough time. What you have to do, is be honest about your problem, and let your audience know you are aware of all the aspects of your problem but have confined your research to this one narrow piece of it. Otherwise, they won't believe any of it."

What she was saying made an impact on all of us as we struggled with defining the problems we were going to tackle. But I was watching the casual way she could rest her lovely ass on the edge of the table, one foot swinging gently, the other supporting her on the floor. In quieter moments she straddled the corner of the table as if riding a horse, at other times she was sitting in the center, always leaning intently into the area between her and the class. And all this when she wasn't pacing back and forth. None of this was feminine, yet I could concentrate on nothing but what was under that skirt. Her skirts were always long enough so not much of her legs showed in any of her activity; still I fantasized about the pleasures and delights that were possible at the upper ends of those legs.

I can't say exactly what it was that intrigued me about her. And I can't explain why she was a sexual turn-on, but I was consumed with lustful thoughts about her. Understand she had given me no reason; I recognized that it was all in my head, but still I projected myself into her life about which I knew nothing and often sat in her classes with an erection.

Fortunately, our text was large and heavy.

CHAPTER FOUR

A nd then it was six months later. Tina had sent us a sign-up sheet for half-hour conferencing appointments. They would have to go from four till ten o'clock so she could see each one of us individually. There were twelve of us left in the class.

I had been promoted three months before, and I had a new manager. So far he seemed like one of the good guys, and we were on that learning curve everyone talks about. He was learning how far he could push me, and I was learning everything I could about this new job. And I had a lot to learn.

I was energized by the more managerial tasks he assigned to me. We both realized I was better with the people side than he was. So I spent a lot of time on personnel problems which he ignored. He came out of the finance side of the house and I don't know if that background dissipates creativity or if he just never had any. And then there were the production problems. I was trying to put what I learned into use—thinking out of boxes, but mostly he thought in columns—of figures.

So instead of my former eight hours, I frequently stayed late which created some problems at home, but more money had a way of quieting Anna's squabbling about it. Three months later, she seemed to have adjusted. I had tried not to abuse this newly found peace between us and suggested she get involved with the Croatian Ethnic Club in the city because it would give her that "outlet" everyone was always saying women who didn't work needed. And that turned out to be a God's send. They had some activities for the kids as well as some political speakers whom I enjoyed. And Anna found some new friends, quit depending on me for everything.

I had met Anna at just such a group in Monrovia, California, the first American city I lived in. I was not looking for a wife, but I guess if anyone had asked me, I would have said that if I were looking for a wife, I would want her to be Croatian. I wasn't looking for a wife because I still hadn't gotten over my first love, Nadja, who was still in Dubrovnik. I guess. I haven't heard from her since we parted.

Nadja and I had been childhood sweethearts, running around the walls and stony hills of Dubrovnik in our bare feet. She made me laugh and feel carefree from the time we were children. We had shared our childhood and later our early teens. Then it didn't seem impossible to put our dreams together, even though we both knew my goal was to emigrate to America and hers was never to leave Dubrovnik. Maybe each of us thought the other would give in and adopt the other dream. That didn't happen. When I left to go to school in Zagreb, she chose to stay in Dubrovnik; and when I was ready to leave Zagreb to come to America, she was not and would not. We were both nineteen.

Life in Yugoslavia has never been easy, and there are the nationalists, like Russians, who think the Mother Country is sacred and holy and who would never leave. Then there are the others who are continually searching. I am one of them although I love my native country with a passion. I am still trying to merge my feelings for my homeland, which will never leave me, with my feelings for America, my adopted country which I also love. Sometimes it is a great puzzle to me how much I love this country, and how annoyed I can be with it. But in all honesty, I was the same in Croatia—much as I loved my country, I was critical of it.

Anna was born here of parents who had emigrated in the forties after the second World War. From family stories and history texts at school, I can understand why someone would want to leave then—relatives on opposite sides of political ideologies, neighbors suspicious of neighbors, a country torn apart by the upheaval of war-time unrest.

There was no chance of her wanting to go live in Zagreb—or Dubrovnik for that matter. She was barely interested in her parents' native country. She was an American. But she had been reared by Croatian parents with the values they brought with them. And we both understood what those were: loyalty, honesty, love of country (whichever one, or all three in my case, since I count Greece among them), hard work and no complaining.

But Anna was an American and had learned to complain in spite of her upbringing. So it was a struggle to give her the happiness she thought she deserved.

I had signed up for the last slot on Tina's schedule because I knew I could get at the pile of work on my desk. And then Carol, one of my study team mates, stopped in early to remind me that it was Tina's birthday and we had decided to buy her some flowers. "Okay, I'll take care of it," I promised.

"My appointment's not 'till nine thirty."

I waited to see how she had fared because I knew Carol was un-prepared. She was sniffling when she came out, but said, "She's go-ing to work with me, gave me some ideas on managing my time. But I've got to go—the counseling session." So we left for the parking lot together; Carol to go off to one more family counseling session, and I to find a place to buy flowers. I went to the closest place I could think of—a nearby hospital where I found a gift shop still open. Three red roses seem just right—not too showy or embarrassing, but enough to say, "We think you're special and happy birthday."

Perhaps it was because my house was full of noisy relatives from Greece; perhaps I was suffering from a mid-life crisis early; perhaps I really wanted to get closer to Tina; I don't know why. But after signing Carol's and my name to the florist's card, I turned it over and wrote a poem that had just run through my mind from my teen years when I spent the summer in Greece with my paternal grand-parents. So I wrote it in Greek.

We were still discussing some additional ideas I wanted to pursue in my project when the security guy came to lock up. As we gathered up our papers and she took the vase with the roses, I realized I didn't want to end our conversation. I told myself it was still about my project, but I don't really think that's honest. I had been sitting next to Tina for a half hour now, and although I thought I knew how she would smell, the reality was quite another thing. Those thoughts I had about her when I was farther away sitting at one of those tables were now like cotton candy in the carnival of my mind—stuck there on the roller coaster twirling and looping around, but stuck even on the more innocent merry-go-round.

I wanted more, any way I could get it, so I said, "Look, if I buy you a drink, could I buy a little more of your time? I still have some questions, and it is your birthday..."

She hesitated, and I thought, "Sasha, you fool!"

But after a moment's pause, she agreed.

So I finally had her all to myself. I was careful to keep the discussion on my paper initially, and then, somehow, we ended up pleasantly arguing over whether burning the flag should be outlawed.

I hadn't sat like this with an interesting, intelligent woman for a long time. And whatever sensual thoughts I harbored about Justina Packard, I knew for sure she would titillate me mentally and intellectually for a long time. Nonetheless, I have to admit glimpses of her black-stockinged legs, which she had tucked up under her on the couch where we sat and drank, aroused erotic thoughts rather than intellectual ones.

I walked her to her car and waited while she unlocked it. She turned to say goodnight, and impulsively I hugged her—a friendly hug—although God knows I was aching for something more. Aghast at myself, I mumbled something like, "Thank you for everything... and happy birthday."

She smiled and touched my arm. "Just do a good job on that project." And she climbed into her little car and drove away.

I was going to be home much later than usual, although Anna knew I had this nine thirty appointment, but whatever the price, I would pay it. As I drove off, I kept playing over the evening in my mind, alternately smiling and cursing myself for the stupid things I had said. Home was ten miles away, and the sooner I got there, the better off I'd be, but again, I found myself wanting to drive on by my own house and seek out the pleasure of the lake so as not to break the silence around me nor let go of the conversation and laughter in my head. Was this joy? I didn't know.

CHAPTER FIVE

It was our last night of class with Tina. There was rejoicing among the twelve of us who were still left. Tina never let a student withdraw if there was any way at all to save him (or her). She had pushed and pulled Carol through, knowing what was going on in her family, with Carol's papers and phone calls going back and forth between them. And Carol rose to the occasion with help from the rest of us as well—early morning meetings before work when she distributed her questionnaire and we acted as her respondents and critiqued it; lunch times when we read her literature review and made suggestions. It was a matter of loyalty among us, not to have one of our team drop out.

Tina was bright and smiling when we gathered, and I realized that she frequently worked eleven- and twelve-hour days. Yet, whenever I saw her, she gave no evidence that she had been working that kind of day. Perhaps it was her energy that separated her from the rest of our professors. They usually came dragging in looking and acting as tired and bedraggled as we were after a day's work.

I never heard her complain in all the time we were together—not about being tired, or about her work, and only vaguely (and that rarely) about her life as she tried to explain her affair with me to me. Actually, I didn't want to know and didn't even care for a long time, but it was important for her (as it seems to be for most women) that I didn't think she was promiscuous and easy. Promiscuous, I never thought, but easy? She was the easiest woman to make love to that I ever knew.

I mean that in the most complimentary way. She was as honest in bed as she was in real life. That was pretty disconcerting at first. Most women I've slept with are different in bed from how you anticipate, and I've never been able to predict how it's going to go. Some lead you on and you think they will be tigers in bed. And you find out they're doing what they do best when they're leading you on—just teasing—and it goes flat. Others turn coy, or shy, or cold. But Justina Packard enjoyed sex the way I did. She was curious and inventive, yet she was strangely innocent in the beginning for someone her age. But she was what she liked to refer to as a "quick study."

"Tell me, Sasha, tell me."

And I answered, "You tell me."

And she said, "I don't even know." And amid her sighs and low moans, she whispered, "Just keep doing what you're doing."

We talked about our loving before and after without ever losing the magic and wonder of what we did; sometimes she still lay on top of me, her breath warm and moist and coming in gasps, her body slightly damp, and I knew how she felt: to move would have plummeted us back to earth where neither of us wanted to return. And so we lay quietly, bonded to each other like a laminate, even breathing as one.

Time was our only enemy—there was never enough.

That last night of our class, when she asked me to translate the poem on the back of the florist's card, I was embarrassed. I couldn't imagine what I was thinking when I wrote it. Of course, she would want to know what it said…

We went off to the Coq d'Or again, because we hadn't finished discussing my paper. I was searching for a strategy to deal with my manager. I felt certain I was going to be sand-bagged by him, the guy who came from finance and was a numbers person, because my project was dedicated to exactly that. And he had never thought to investigate our particular numbers, just accepted the status quo. New to the job and wanting to make a mark for myself, I wanted to combine this class project, which was required for graduation, with improving production.

When I presented the idea to him, he was all gung-ho—thought it was a great idea, saw benefits to the department. Later, when I expanded it to include a cost analysis of the various areas I was studying, I could feel his reluctance, and it was then I realized that he didn't want me to get credit for it because it was something he should have already done. But since the project proposal had already been approved by him and his manager, he was stuck with me and my project.

So the atmosphere changed in the office. It was little things—memos that he didn't pass on and the "surprise" that I hadn't gotten the information in them, meetings in which he had before frequently deferred to me were now conducted as if I weren't even there. There was nothing to actually sabotage the work, just a shift in our relationship that I became very aware of.

I study people carefully; I've had to, to survive, and I can feel when people change before there's any noticeable change in their behavior. And maybe that's what happened that night. I felt Justina soften and warm to me even though nothing seemed to have changed in her behavior.

I was playing with my keys which I had left on the table and I could hear their familiar sound. It's funny how everyone's keys have that certain sound their owner can identify. I heard the metals rubbing and softly clanging and I wanted to stop but I couldn't, and over this slight cacophony, I mumbled through a translation of the poem and saw her flush, but she quickly recovered. "That's sad and poignant, but very lovely." She looked up in some confusion and asked, "How old were you when you wrote it?" And then quickly looked down again not wanting to look at me when I answered.

"Probably sixteen or seventeen—I don't really remember." She was quiet as she played with the cocktail napkin under her wine glass, folding up the edges around the stem. My emotions when I wrote that poem rose up now into my throat, and I realized I was feeling them now for this woman. Dammit, why did I ever write that to her? You are such an ass, Sasha. Now look what you've done.

She shifted in her seat and turned to the discussion of my project. And I thought, "Okay, you're saved from further embarrassment."

I ordered another round of drinks because we were now deep

into other discussions. I watched her listen intently to whatever I said as she thought about our conversation and responded, and finally, she relaxed enough to fold her legs up under her and turn her whole body to me instead of looking straight ahead and merely turning her head.

Part of the time, some dark corner of my mind was coldly calculating my chances to score, and I was mentally rehearsing the moves that had been successful in the past. But the better part of me was ignoring those. Even then I knew that anything that might have succeeded in the past was not going to work with her.

I had thought about this woman for so long that even laying my hand softly on her knee to make a point just seemed natural. She didn't withdraw or pretend to be shocked, and we continued on as if I hadn't touched her. I didn't move my hand. But in some way, it all changed, not at that particular moment, but slowly. Everything else vanished. I knew there were other people in the room, but not for me. She was the only person there.

When the waiter came to ask if we wanted another round, it was an intrusion, and she shook her head, "No." We sat silently, waiting for the bill, and I tried not to look at the wedding band on her finger as she resumed creasing and folding that soggy napkin around the stem of her wine glass. What was she thinking? My heart was thumping in my chest. How could I let her go? How could I not? I paid the bill, she smiled at the waiter, and we left.

I wanted to pick her up, take her back to the classroom and set her on one of those tables where she so often sat, and I had so often daydreamed about her. I wanted to kneel before the altar of her furry crotch where those legs ended. But we ended up in her car, one of us on either side of the console and shift of that silly little car.

It has always seemed very strange to me: I never felt as if I had made a conquest that night. Instead it was as if she had given me this treasure which was herself, and I felt as if that treasure had been given to me to cherish and keep safe.

Later when we talked about that night, I asked her why she let me kiss her that first time. We were in bed and she stared up at the ceiling for a long time. Finally, she said slowly, "I'll never know, Sasha. I'll never know."

She lay absolutely quiet. Then, "You were a hurricane pounding at my doors and windows nailed shut against the elements when I didn't even expect a storm. And one by one the windows burst open and you blew through this house where I lived so safely, so peacefully—shards and debris from that life airborne—and I guess I suddenly wanted to know how it was to live some other way—with the wind blowing through the rooms and the sunshine streaming in the windows, the sheer curtains blowing mysteriously—see what I didn't know, what had eluded me."

We were quiet as I thought about her description—I could hear her quiet breathing slow and melodious to my ear, and I realized as we lay there quietly, our hearts as well as our bodies once again one, that for me she was the eye of the hurricane—a kind of dangerous quiet and peace for me to explore before the other side of the storm whipped around bringing disaster.

After I left her that night, I had to take the extra time to stop at a gas station and wash up. Bad enough to be late, and this was really late; no reason to give Anna even the scent of suspicion. For all the times I've been accused without reason, at least this time I was guilty. Still, why give her the aroma of another woman to justify those suspicions?

I never asked Justina how she managed at home that night. And she never asked me. For as much as we bared our bodies and our souls to each other, probed the recesses of the other's mind, there were some things we always left unspoken—those deceitful things that would have reminded us of what we were doing.

CHAPTER SIX

Hen I called her the next morning to make sure she was all right, she said she was feeling fragile… "Very fragile." Such a word for this woman! I wondered what it meant then, but later as we grew to know each other, I found that fragile side of her appealing. There was almost nothing about her that wasn't appealing as time went on, but still she scared me.

She was freer and more open than any person I had ever known. I didn't know how to accept that gift yet, and I didn't even know if I could learn. I had to believe she was real first. So I tested in subtle ways. I didn't call. She said she understood, wanted only what I wanted to give, didn't want a call because I thought I had to, but only those made out of desire. And I wondered how long that would last before she was screaming and demanding more.

If she was real, would I grow to love her, learn what love is, and become even more dissatisfied than I am now? Undoubtedly, she intruded into my life by presenting other possibilities. If I stayed in my box, convinced those possibilities did not exist, could not exist, I could tolerate who I am, what I have.

If I realize there can be more, what will I do?

A few years ago it was popular to immerse oneself in a cylinder of body temperature water and silence to commune with yourself. It is one of those strange American fads, but that silence, that peace is what I crave, and I don't know how to accomplish it. My life is whirling around me; always it seems as if a small, non-destructive bomb has gone off and pieces are sailing though the air attacking me at will, paper airplanes thrust by an unseen hand. I have no control.

Shrapnel from home, debris from my job, even dreams from my youth bombard me with enough momentum so that I feel their impact; then they slide off and lay at my feet before I've had a chance to examine them fully, to decide what they mean, what to do about them.

I am drawn to Justina and her freedom, but she is another knife in my side from which I feel yet more of my energy slowly ooze. She provides me with the only humor, the only joy I know. And so she is more to be feared than the rest.

We've talked about Maslow's hierarchy of needs in my classes. To be self actualized!—to have the presence, the guiltlessness to try for that. I only know obligation, responsibility. That she presents a different view—that she is close to it—is more frightening to me than she can imagine. If such actualization is possible, I am so far away in thought and deed. I don't know this willful search for self.

Perhaps it is possible only for Americans who were brought into this world with the idea that anything is possible. Greeks are fatalistic. They live with the evidence that anything is possible, but everything is tenuous. One day (or century) you are number one, the next, your empire has crumbled. And for all my love of Croatia, its history has provided more potent and oppressive lessons. Am I a victim of my history, my culture, my genes?

I want to keep her with me. I recognize that she is the most important part of my life; not my daily life as I live it, but my inner life as I conceive it. I worry that I won't be able to give her what she needs, don't know how to let go of this black cloud that consumes me. So I wait.

I once told her I was as patient as a donkey—I could wait—for her, for the opportunities to be with her. She said, "More like a mule—stubborn. We are opposite. I have no patience. I work for what I want when I identify whatever that is. And then I want it now. Later, whenever that is, whatever it is, will be something else. That's a given. Time does a number on everything."

And our timing was awful. No, my timing was awful!

At the outset, my house which is always full anyway, was even more crowded with relatives from Greece—my brother, his wife, and their three kids were visiting. The original plan was for them to come two weeks before Christmas and stay for two more weeks. His business in Salonika was self-sufficient: cousins and uncles could take care of everything in his absence. But they did such a good job, that the month-long visit lasted nine weeks. Nine long weeks when Anna bitched into the little privacy we had, granny suffered congestive heart failure and refused later treatments, and my home was turned into a noisy circus with friends and relatives visiting our guests as well.

I miss those two countries—Greece and Croatia—where I grew up. But I find that some of things I liked most about them then are the very things that I now find annoying: the acceptance by family and friends that you will always be there to help them and the hurt feelings if you can't or don't want to. Maybe I've become so American that I am moving more and more toward self-sufficiency and no longer enjoy the exchanged benefits from those relationships, don't find the rewards I once did in the extended family. My family already seems more than I bargained for.

I am eager for quiet and peace, for some absolute silence of my own, a space where I can exist as me. Yet every such moment is sucked up by someone around me, including Justina. While she gives me pleasure, brings me laughter, she is still another intrusion in my life. And I wonder at the quality of my life and what I am willing to put up with when I can say that and know it is true. Worse yet, I have this sense of internal isolation that never lets up—that I can't release, can't open up to let anyone in.

It has been too long since I trusted anyone, let alone this strange, exotic woman who loves me, loves to make love to me, cares about me, goes out of her way to do things for me. I don't know how to accept her gifts—I have no experience, so in my ineptitude, I become ungracious, or so it must seem to her. The only times in my life others have done something good for me is when they wanted something in return, usually more than they gave, or so it seems to me. She wants only to shower down the sunshine of her affection, but even that I can't return in kind or as I'd like to. I don't know how to accept her joy—what will be demanded of me later?

So I withdraw. I retreat. I am afraid.

If I learn to live and love this way, how will I tolerate my life? Is it possible to live this way? And if it's possible, not just some craziness in my head, I have already wasted my best years, tolerated a life which I made that is damaging and unhealthy. No wonder she frightens me!

But this is my internal life. On the outside, everything is as usual…

CHAPTER SEVEN

Justina talks a lot about boxes and circles, the differences in the ways men and women perceive their lives and then live them. My best friend and colleague, Michael, lives in the worst kind of box; he is paralyzed from the waist down. Although wheel-chair bound, he has found some kind of peace that I have not. Strange to say, but in some ways I envy him—not, of course his paralysis, but his nobility in dealing with it.

He started the undergraduate program after I did and he is in Justina's class now. In the way of lovers who want to know everything about the other and to get someone else's point of view, I asked Michael for a drink so I could talk about her without revealing my relationship with her, hear about her from someone else. We met at a bar not far from the plant.

Although Michael is my best friend, there was no way I could say to him, "Justina Packard and I are lovers." Once and only once I trusted a friend with a secret, and although it was innocent and not deliberate nor malicious, he betrayed me. I vowed never again to reveal a secret to anyone.

Instead, I asked, "So, how's school going?"

"Great. I love it. I never thought I'd say that about going to school. I never was a good student you know." He was quiet and sipped his beer slowly. "Maybe this," and he looked down at his legs, "and all the learning I've had to do to accept it has made me a better student in all areas of my life. D'ya think?" It was a question that didn't require a response. And we were both quiet for a few moments.

"Anyway, when I finish—if I ever finish, there'll be some other opportunities available. Maybe I can get out of that madhouse back there or find some other job within it that will be a challenge. I've always had the feeling I was hired because I was disabled. You know, 'How many cripples do we need to fill our quota?' and I appeared on the scene at the right time." His laugh was self-deprecating and he paused. Then, "I'm not complaining exactly, but I guess I am, too. Fuck, I might not even be as well off as I am if I weren't tied to this chair. I might have blown away my whole life instead of having to face up to it.

"Ya' know, Sasha, a physical paralysis is not the greatest disability of them all. I see so many people around me who are mental cripples, emotional cripples…" and his voice trailed off, and he looked directly at me.

"Whoa! You think I'm one of them?"

"Ummm, getting there—probably borderline. I see you failing yourself, your potential. Especially within the past two years, I see you with less of that spark—that edge—sort of weary and tired all the time, and cranky and angry some of the time. Those are not the marks of a healthy man, my friend."

I scowled at him. I was angry and hurt, and he must have seen my expression change. So before I could say anything, he continued kindly, "But I also notice some slight change in you recently—not a renewal exactly, but some movement toward the humor you seemed to have lost."

Michael raised his eyebrows slightly, questioning. When I didn't respond, he tried to soften his earlier condemnation. He adopted a tone of camaraderie and leaned across the table. "When we were first friends, I was happy to be around your craziness and your laughter and your energy. You were always looking for a 'trip', you know? The funny side of everything, and then you'd make it even funnier with your sarcasm. Slowly, that went away, as if that side of you has been smothered by the cares of I don't know what—your job? your family? school? I hope it isn't school. I don't want that to happen to me." Michael had left his keys on the table and was making designs with the pointed end of one on his coaster. I knew he was uncomfortable because I remembered that night with Justina when I could hear myself playing with my keys and couldn't stop.

"And I needed you to be my friend then, just because you had this not-everything-is-serious side to you when I needed to be able to make fun of things, including myself. Now I feel as if I've gone beyond where you were then, or you're going backward. Your—what's the word—exuberance? If it's not gone, it sure is diminished."

What could I say? I felt the same thing myself until Justina. But I couldn't tell him about her. And Michael was on a roll...

"Where did it go? Where do those joyful parts of us go when they leave? I read a poem once about joy, as if it was a tangible thing you could pluck—held high like the brass ring at the merry-go-round, waiting for someone who recognized it to ride by on his horse and reach up and grab it. That was pretty potent for me. I tried to imagine myself in my wheelchair being able to do that.

"Then one day I was out in the park exercising and I watched some dandelion fuzzies flying by above my head. Do you have dandelions in Greece and Croatia?" When I nodded, he continued, "Remember how when we were kids, we'd blow off the seeds while they were still on the stem and watch them fly away in the wind? I wanted to do that.

"I wheeled around the park until I found one still growing that I could reach and bent over to pick it. I was all alone, and I sat there like a six-year-old blowing the seed fuzzies off that stem into the air. They were all airborne and flying away, except one, which for some reason, hovered just in front of me. I reached out my hand to catch it before it, too, flew away.

"As a grown-up, have you ever really looked at one of those? It was so delicate and beautiful—so little substance, yet so perfect. I remembered that poem, and I knew I had captured for a few seconds some joy—unplanned unanticipated, unknown until that moment.

"When I blew it off my outstretched palm so it could join its sisters in the breeze, some part of me flew away with it. My body was wheelchair bound; my spirit took a ride. I was happy for those few moments, moments I would never have had if I weren't in this chair." I could see he was embarrassed at revealing so much of himself, so I said nothing. But having started, he finished.

"I think about that dandelion occasionally, both at the low times and the high times in my life. I know that such simple pleasures are possible if you recognize them. They're powerful. So when I'm down, I remember that there are those other moments like that still waiting for me; and when I'm up, I add those moments to the treasures I've stored in my dandelion box. My body is in this wheelchair, but where I live is in my head, and at those times I can even forget the physical constraints I endure. I guess everyone lives in a wheelchair of his own choosing."

What could I say? We ordered another beer, but the mood had been broken. He sounded like Justina—optimists that they both were. Maybe that's why I liked them both so much. The thought of her gave me the chance to change the subject when the beers arrived.

"So, how's school?" I tried again. "Which class are you in?" As if I didn't know.

"Great. I'm in Org Behavior with a woman, Justina Packard." Don't call her Justina, I wanted to shout. I am the only one who calls her by her given name.

But in a natural voice, I asked, "How do you like her?" afraid the conversation would end there.

"Don't know for sure, yet. She's different from anyone else we've had. We have to work harder for her, but it's funny, nobody minds. We all want to work harder to please her. It's 'Do you think she'll like this?' or 'Let's really do a bang-up job on this presentation.'— as if we had to meet her standards. Yet she keeps telling us to set our own standards, to decide what it is we want to learn and go for it. I'm still trying to figure her out—whether she's manipulating us or if she's really sincere in wanting to set us free in the classroom. It's powerful." Then curiously, "Did you have her?"

Did I have her? Every which way. Upside down, standing, sitting on the edge of the table, bent over, almost inside out. By now I know every crevice, every fold in her body. Did I have her? Oh, Michael, if you only knew, you'd be happy for me. But I said, "Yeah, I had her for Org Behavior, too, and for Business Research. She's sincere; enjoy her; she's one of a kind."

"Yeah, I notice that former students are always hanging around her. All our classes aren't in the plant, you know, and when we're at the university, no matter where she goes, there are students, not even from our class, trying to have conversations with her, letting her know what's going on. She's the huggiest, kissiest person I ever saw with them." He grinned wickedly, "I can hardly wait to be one of her former students to cash in."

I was stunned. I wanted to hit my best friend. "She's not like that at all," I said quietly, but there must have been something in my voice for Michael laughed crudely and obscenely. "Oho! What have we here? A crush on the 'teach'?"

I took a swig of my beer to cover my anger and confusion, and into it my best friend, Michael peered.

"Oh God, Sasha. I'm sorry. I had no idea. But that explains a lot. Those subtle changes, your contemplativeness, the telephone calls when you close the door. Oh, God, I'm sorry."

"Sorry? Why do you keep saying you're sorry. Sorry for what? What is explained? Michael, you are going mad." I had recovered and needed to redirect this conversation.

But Michael was not going to leave it there. "Okay, okay, Sasha. But I am sorry. She's much more my type than yours. You will only bring each other grief. You, because you can't give her anything— right now you have nothing left over to give anybody. And she'll bring you grief, too, because she'll try to show you the way and you are too fuckin' stubborn to open your eyes." I said nothing, and he continued, "Still, some of it will get through to you, which will be even worse.

"If I had two working legs, I'd fight you for her. As it is, all I an do is just sit here in my chair and wait. It may be all I can do."

Michael was my best friend because he never pulled any punches, but I hated him momentarily. And I hated him profoundly at that moment because I knew what he said had the ring of truth. And even though I couldn't, wouldn't promise Justina anything beyond whatever moment we were in, I couldn't stand the thought of Michael, of anyone, knowing her intimately, having her, being capable of giving her more than I could.

CHAPTER EIGHT

I was driving my truck and Justina was directing me. We were to have a picnic in the mountains. I thought I knew almost every major road in our state, but here we were on a road I didn't even know existed. It was not paved, and the gravel was a different kind of symphony as it bounced against the wheel housings marking our journey. It was not unpleasant, just a reminder that we were on a treacherous road. Off in the distance I could see the sacred mountain Justina frequently referred to—a wide-based cone with a curious ridge around its pointed tip.

"Whenever I see that mountain, I always think of it as a boob," I said.

Justina giggled. "Of course, why do you think I brought you here? You and your symbolism… I knew you'd like it, and we'd have a wonderful afternoon.

"Actually, the turn-off to go around the mountain isn't even as good as this, but that's the only way you can get to the top. It's an old Indian trail, but passable without any trouble in the truck. I've done it once by myself in the car, so it's do-able."

"You drove on this road by yourself?" I was shocked.

"Of course. Why not? Who would stop me if I wanted to do it? An Indian elder told me about it when I was working on the reservation, so I tried to find it when I had a day off and nothing to do—the same Indian elder who taught me to chop wood, incidentally." She was dreamy for a few moments. Then she continued, "He was very fond of me, and he had no preconceived notions about women's capabilities or their safety, believing as he does in the rightness of the earth. If I had died, he would not have felt guilt about giving me the information—he would have known it was my destiny to die on that sacred mountain."

We drove straight on; quiet, soft music on the tape, gravel ricocheting against the metal of the truck; Justina, soft by my side. The mountain lost some of its breast-like quality as we neared it. I like to think of myself as adventurous, but I was uncomfortable driving on a road I had never been on before, didn't know, one not even paved. When I told this to Justina, she laughed. "Darling, we are both on a road we have never been on before."

I turned to her quickly. "I thought you said you had been here before?"

"Oh, the street-road; of course I have been. I told you that. I meant the symbolic road we are on. It's all a gamble, isn't it? Wondering what we'll find at the end?" She moved closer and laid her head lightly on my shoulder, slipped her sun-warmed hand behind my back and down into the back of my jeans. "Always the possibility of a surprise... You don't much like surprises, do you, Sasha?"

"No. The surprises I've had in my life have all been unpleasant ones. I've never had a surprise birthday party or anything else that was unexpected and pleasant. In fact, even the things I've planned, maybe especially the things I've planned, haven't worked out well. That's why I hate planning. I anticipate the pleasure and get the pain."

She couldn't resist. "Even me?"

"The jury is still out on you, my sweet. I still don't believe you're real. If you were what you seem to be, why would you be here with me?"

Her face darkened and her voice turned hard. She moved away and took her hand out of my jeans. "Sasha, you are talking about someone I love, and I never let anyone disparage those I love in my presence. If you choose to harbor that image of yourself, keep it to yourself." Her eyes filled with unshed tears. And then she turned scolding...

"After all the times we've been together, I can't believe you are still putting yourself down that way. One of these days I'll be so weary of hearing it, I'll let my guard down and begin to believe you. You know if we send ourselves and others messages often enough, we all begin to believe them. What I don't understand is why we all prefer to send and receive negative messages instead of positive ones." When I didn't answer, she finally said, "Whatever... I just don't want to be the receiver."

We were at the base of the mountain, and Justina warned me to slow down because the turn-off was not obvious. Once again, I was doubtful about this journey, but soon, she spied a landmark. "There," she pointed. "Now around that turn is the greenest tree I have ever seen. I saw it first around this time of the day in Spring, too. I had to stop to take it in; it hurt so to look at it amidst all this tan and brown. I thought it was a lesson about nature's ability to endure even when the environment is hostile."

The tree sprang into view as we made the curve. It was that shade of green that is almost all light, and with the sun on it, I felt I had to squint to avoid the assault to my eyes.

We drove on in silence, not an angry one, but she didn't move back to where she had been. She was lost in thought, and I was concentrating on the road. We were on the very narrow dirt road she had warned me about, and we drove around and around the mountain on that dirt trail worn into its side, going higher and higher. The going wasn't rough, it was slow. And it was breathtaking.

Justina was calmer, more at peace now, and as I drove carefully, I imagined her driving this alone in that silly car of hers, never knowing what was ahead. Frequently, there wasn't even a place where I could make a U-turn.

"What were you thinking when you came up here that first time?" I asked.

She thought for a while as the music played. "I guess I was thinking that this road is so much like life. It goes round and round; some of it's rocky and some of it's smooth; some of it's pretty ordinary and some of it is exquisitely beautiful. Look at that tree!" And she pointed to another lone tree which was bathed in sunlight. And as we passed, she continued, "But I knew if I made the crest, then perhaps I would be able to fly, to soar, to know." She looked at me to see if I understood.

"And?"

She was quiet again. "This is where I learned to let go. Before I was always fighting myself." Then, softly, "Like you do." And she turned warm toward me again. "I don't know if it will work for you. Maybe you have to come here alone, be alone, and my being here will spoil it for you. But now you will know how to get here if you ever want to..."

We finally arrived at the summit. Neither of us spoke. I turned off the engine, and we sat there, silent, neither of us inclined to move or speak, much as we had that first night in her car.

I took her hand and kissed it, and she lifted our clasped hands to her lips and held them there. I lifted our two hands to my lips once again, then got out of the truck and came around and opened her door. She put her hand into mine and got out, and we walked, still mute, to a level spot in the sun where we sat. There was a gentle breeze, but I could still hear humming through the brush as it passed over and around us.

She turned her face to me; quiet tears slid down her face. And I took her in my arms and we loved each other then in the softest, gentlest way possible. She was there for me with all her earthly flesh, but she was ethereal in some way. I felt as if I had touched her very soul, so delicate was she. And still the quiet tears poured out of her. I kissed them from her cheeks and hesitated, and she whispered, "Please don't stop, Sasha, it feels like forever. I'm sorry about the tears, I just can't stop them."

I could not have stopped loving her then any more than she could stop the tears. I never wanted to stop, wanted to hold these moments captive, to savor them, never to climax, only to anticipate that moment. But eventually, we lay as one.

I felt her breathing become quieter, felt the rhythm of her body, her heart. I thought I really could touch her soul, hold it in my hand if only I were gentle enough. And still the tears came. She did not sob; there was no other evidence of her crying. I continued to kiss them from her cheeks, but the ones I drank up so greedily were soon replaced with fresh ones.

I wanted to take her into my body as she had so often taken me into hers—to have that same sense of having her with me always that I imagined she had—to see if I could recreate these moments at will from the cells of my memory wherever and whenever I needed her. But I could not say the words to her.

Finally, we slept there on the mountaintop. I had a moment when I looked down at us from above, when I could see us as we lay there, but I couldn't see where she ended and I began and I went back to sleep at peace, safe and secure.

We awoke, slightly sweaty, around noon. She rose up, stretched her arms skyward, and said calmly, "I think I'll fly. Do you want to come with?" She had this funny way of leaving off the "me" when inviting me to go someplace with her.

"Sure. Where'll we go?"

"Oh, just around—survey things. See how we're doing.""

"Let's go." I played along with her.

She folded her jeans and her shirt and out of the picnic basket, she took a short, white satin shirt with full sleeves and put that on.

I watched, fascinated. She was great at putting on shows for me—sometimes dressing up. In her picnic basket were always a bottle of wine, some cheeses and crackers or bread and some smoked meats. She also always had candles, two beautiful stemmed glasses and an assortment of lingerie, silk scarves, other things for fun. Once even a pair of play handcuffs. "In case we want to be keenky," she teased, sounding just like me. Sometimes we used some of the stuff; other times we never even looked into the basket. So I waited.

She kissed me profoundly as if she were saying good-bye and looked deeply into my eyes. "Did I ever tell you your eyes are the color of used copper—not the brassy color of shiny, new copper, but copper with the patina of the centuries. I love your eyes, Sasha; I love you, Sasha. Can you come with, do you think?" And she pulled me to my feet.

I looked into the basket. "Where's my flying shirt?"

She put the lid down. "Oh, you have to earn your shirt. The first time you have to be willing to go as you are."

She walked to the edge as if to step off, and instead she calmly spread her arms and soared skyward. She looked back once and beckoned to me, then she was off—sometimes a mere speck in the blue, dipping and diving, soaring and reaching new heights. The wind echoed her last words. "We are all alone; that's what freedom is."

"Justina," I cried. "Come back." I knew I could not go where she went. Try as she might, she could not help me. Try as I might, I could not go. I was not ready; not either with her nor for her could I make the leap. I was an earthling, fettered and bound by my own doing, kept there only by myself. Perhaps that was the lesson I was meant to learn there on the sacred mountain.

I looked down from above again and saw myself, alone, arms stretched up and out, wanting to fly with her while my feet were chained to a tree with a huge boulder entwined within the chains. I knew I had to release myself; at the same time I saw how impossible that was likely to be. But I had to make the attempt. I watched from above as you can do in dreams, trying to loosen myself from those constraints.

The chains made a great racket, clanging and dropping as I fought to release myself. They moved and slithered around the boulder and across the ground, and I saw what seemed to be a weak link here, and there! a lock with the key still protruding. I writhed and wrenched my body; I was bent double, searching, reaching for either of those sections of chain which would set me free, when a large unseen hand grabbed me by the shoulder and hauled me backward, keeping me from the prize.

"For God's sake, wake up. You'll have the whole house awake." And Anna turned over and went back to sleep.

But I lay awake until morning.

CHAPTER NINE

Finally! Only six more weeks of classes before graduation. We were all excited. This was it! Our research projects had been submitted and graded. Fortunately, the grades were awarded by committee, much to Justina's relief.

Some had said they weren't going to march in the commencement exercises—they just wanted the piece of paper; others said they wouldn't miss it after how hard they had worked. But eventually, everyone in our group did participate.

When my phone rang that morning right after that last class started, I was sitting in my office, and I was hoping it was Justina since I was shifting gears and hadn't started on a report that was due. I was thinking about her then, not as my lover, but as my professor, trying to remember the lessons on writing techniques about which she was such a bear: Just the facts, no weasely adjectives, no "I believes," just the who-what-where-when-why-how and how much. But I could never think about Justina in that role for very long any more. Immediately, other visions intruded, even her flying in that satin blouse in my dream.

I picked it up on the second ring, "This is Sasha."

The voice on the other end said, "Is Alexander Psipsopoulos there?"

I am so rarely called Alexander, that I had a moment's fear—was something wrong? What had happened?

"This is him," and that came out before I had a chance to say it properly. Justina was always annoyed when people didn't say, "This is I—or he—or she."

"Good morning; this is Phelps Morrison, president of Drysdale University." I almost dropped the phone. I could feel myself begin to tremble. All of Justina's fears washed over me. In the same instant I thought, "What can they do to us? They can fire her—they won't let me graduate." But before my fears had a chance to escalate even further, he continued, "I'm calling to congratulate you as the first winner of the Paul Bowers Award. Sooo..." and he hesitated, "Mr. Psipsopoulos (am I pronouncing that correctly?), congratulations! I'd like you to know that you won over several other outstanding candidates, and your plant manager wrote a very complimentary letter outlining the benefits your company has reaped as a result of your project. Good work! You'll receive the award at graduation. You were planning to attend, weren't you?"

I don't know which was worse—the fear or the surprise. So I mumbled something like, "Um, yes, of course, and thank you, sir."

"There will be some publicity on this, so we'll need a short biography from you for the media. Think you could get that to me in a week? You know, something about why you decided to return to school, why you chose Drysdale, how you came to do this particular piece of research, your job, that kind of thing."

"Yes, sir."

And he continued, "Mr. Bowers is here in my office, and he'd like to speak with you. Good luck, Alexander."

And again, all I could mumble was, "Thank you." But I was still trembling, only now from shock.

And then, "Congratulations, Mr. Psipopoulos. This is Paul Bowers. I own Bowers Computer Group and I'm an alumnus of Drysdale. I've been very successful and I owe a lot of it to my own research project at the university, so about a year ago I decided to honor a student who had done an extraordinary job on his or her project and whose company benefited from that project. I'm very pleased to tell you that you are the student who has been chosen by the committee at the university with my very enthusiastic endorsement after reading your project and the letter from your plant manager. You did a fine job. And by the way there is a $500 check that goes with the award."

By now I was recovering. "I'm so surprised I don't know what to say, Mr. Bowers, except thank you very much."

"Just keep up the good work and remember everything you learned at Drysdale. I've found I keep putting it all to good use. All those hours in the classroom and the outside work…"

"Yes, sir."

"Well, I'll see you at graduation, then."

"Yes. And thank you."

I tried hanging up and dropped the phone. I hoped they had already hung up so I didn't injure their eardrums. I didn't want them to figure out they had just made an award to a donkey.

And of course the first thing I thought of was Justina. Justina… jumbled up with all the afternoons and evenings sitting at those rectangular tables, tired, weary, wondering why I was doing this, the other afternoons and evenings with my study team, the papers, the coolness from my boss (Whoa, this will really piss him off.), the image of Justina walking in that first time. I couldn't stop the somersaulting in my head. The plant manager actually knew who I was? But somehow it all came back to Justina—if she hadn't pushed us, if she hadn't been Justina, would I have worked as hard trying to impress anyone else? My head was full of oil and water—the way oil floats like a swirly dark blue and gold rainbow on the top of water—that was Justina. All the rest of it was a dark pool submerged under her color and flash and rhythm as those images tried to break through that iridescent film that was Justina.

As soon as it all stopped and I felt I could speak, I dialed her business number, and got her answering machine. "J. L. Packard and Associates. Please leave a message."

Dammit! She was always there in the morning…

"Well, okay, this is Alexander Psipsopoulos—you know, that name you can't pronounce, the first winner of the Paul Bowers Award." And then I adopted the very formal, business voice of a student. "I'm calling to thank you for putting up with me in class and seeing me through my research project. I couldn't have done it without your help." Dammit, I wanted to talk to her, not her damned machine. "Justina, I need to talk to you, not this machine—tell you in person." And then, because she had left me all those notes. "Call me for a good time."

I sat there in my office for what seemed like a long time—I couldn't tell this morning. Everything was so muddled. I wanted to be with Justina most of all, share this news with her. Finally, I moved. I went to get a cup of coffee hoping I wouldn't have to stop to chat with anyone, but just when you don't want to see anybody, people appear out of the woodwork. Shop talk, gossip, real problems. I didn't want any of it this morning, but I also couldn't cut people off without them thinking something was wrong. Wrong? Everything was so right, I couldn't imagine they didn't see it. I just won the Paul Bowers Award, whatever the hell that is. But it didn't matter. I didn't want to tell anyone yet. Justina had to be the first to know.

When I finally got back to my office, there was her message on my machine in the same voice I had used. "Congratulations, Alexander Psipsopoulos. I can't imagine why you think I still can't pronounce your name. Of course I can. Psipsopoulos. There. And I am very happy for you. You know I had nothing to do with your success; you did it all yourself. Congratulate yourself." And then there was a moment's pause and in the voice I knew so well, "Right now I don't care if your phone is monitored and it's on the PA system blasting all over the plant. I am ecstatic for you, Darling. Where and when should I meet you for the good time you promised?"

I called her back immediately.

"Justina. I was serious. I wouldn't have done that kind of research without you. You know I was trying to impress you, get into your..."

"Sasha, stop. You would have done just as good a job without me—never mind what you were going to say. Do you think that was it? You wouldn't have succeeded with that if I hadn't wanted you to, want you to all the time."

"But you don't know how lazy I can be."

"We can all be lazy. Now about that good time..." And we coordinated our schedules as if it were a business meeting, found a time. Then she said, "Actually I knew your project was among the ones being considered."

"You did? Why didn't you tell me?"

"I wanted to more than you can imagine. But you would have been disappointed if you hadn't won, and besides it would have been a violation of ethics, my dear. I was supposed to be on the selection committee."

"You were on the selection committee?" I was appalled.

"Darling, you weren't listening. I said supposed to be; I asked to be excused when I saw your name on the list."

"What did you say—why you wouldn't?"

"I told them the truth—that I was having an affair with you!" She giggled. "My VP asked for all the details. So I told her everything, Darling, everything—every little detail. She was so scandalized, she decided it would all be better ignored. So she drew up a contract that made me promise to report to her all the details of our trysts, and in exchange she would remain silent and the university's reputation could remain untarnished."

After my initial disbelief, I realized Justina was putting me on. And I gave her some of her own wicked brand of humor.

"So did you tell her about the handcuffs? And how keenky you've become? And how much you love it? I bet she'd like to try it…"

"Sasha, what do you think is the point of the contract I signed? She gets you next—when I have worn you out and not a moment before…"

And then into that awful silence while we both considered what she had just said, "Have you told Anna?"

"No."

"Sasha, call her now. She deserves to know—to share in your pleasure. And I'll see you then. I've got to go find the handcuffs now that you've reminded me of them. Ta Ta." And she was gone without waiting for a reply.

I sat for a few more minutes, the coffee which had smelled so invigorating as I poured it, designed to quiet me somehow, was now cold and unappetizing in front of me, but I sat there smiling at Justina's teasing, shaking my head that she was supposed to be on the selection committee, glad that she wasn't, and finally I dialed my home number.

When I told Anna, she said, "That's nice. What does it mean?"

"Besides the recognition for doing a good job? There were probably more than a couple hundred projects they chose from. Oh, there's $500 that goes with it."

Suddenly, Anna was interested. "$500? Sasha, that's wonderful! Aren't you the clever one? When will you get the money? Soon? Or do we have to wait until graduation?"

"I don't know, Anna; I never asked."

CHAPTER TEN

It had rained earlier in the week, and Spring responded immediately. The desert floor was covered with low-growing wild flowers so profuse it seemed as if they must be carpeting the entire globe. I knew, though, that spring in Zagreb or Salonika did not look like this, and I was melancholy. The desert is not hospitable with its tan and brown landscape, at least not to these eyes used to the blue and the green of my homeland.

There Spring arrives regularly each year with its promises of a new year and re-birth. Even the sea changes color, and the breezes acquire a new scent as they urge the waves to burst upon and recede from the shores. Here in the desert, if there is no rain at just the right moment, suddenly one day it's summer with its intense heat shimmering over the asphalt in waves, and we have endured an entire year of this natural tan, broken only by the masses of blooms put out by the gardeners who import them from other lush places, trying to recreate in this hostile place something from their pasts. Lines for service and check-out on Saturdays and Sundays at the nurseries exceed the lines at the supermarkets, and during the week most of these artificial (in the sense that they're not native) plants require the care of a parent. So strong is the desire to recreate what we have known as children.

On the other hand, there are the orange blossoms here, their scent perfuming the entire city with the smell of innocence and the promise of renewal and fruition. Justina says it is the only time to be in the desert—that even if she lived in the tundra, in March she would still be able to smell the orange blossoms. This woman thinks in smells and aromas and scents the way others think in pictures. So before I even noticed the scent of the orange blossoms, Justina called. "Darling, go outside and inhale." I was in the middle of a project concentrating on a competitor's product, trying to discount the fact that theirs was better than ours in several ways. "I can't. I'm in the middle of comparing two widgets." Justina referred to all of our products as widgets, first of all because so much of it was confidential, the rest of it technical, and neither interested her. She was interested only on a very elementary level because it was my work.

"Darling, I know you. You need a break. Take your great Grecian nose out there and inhale. Then call me back."

"Why? What's going on? What's happening?" I did need a break, but it was always so difficult for me to drop something once I started. I wish I could acquire Justina's ability to operate on several levels at one time, or at least be able to switch back and forth easily. I'm not sure which it is she does. I have learned from the sound of her voice when she answers the phone whether it is a major or minor distraction—the phone—but in either case, within seconds she is purring and humming into my ear, totally concentrating on me. I'm flattered and I wish I could return the favor. But I can't, and frequently she is put off by my inability to get caught up in silliness and/or sex (especially sex) and other emotions when I am working.

I tried to keep her on the phone for a few minutes to create that break, but she wouldn't be held captive. "No. If you have time to talk to me on the phone you can take your lovely backside off that chair, your long Grecian nose out there and inhale as I've asked you to do. Besides I have to go. I know you don't think so, but I work too, and I have a project to finish. But call me back if you get outside. You won't be sorry. Ta Ta, my love." And she hung up.

I worked for a while longer, but my heart was no longer in it. She had piqued my curiosity. I wanted to know what was so important, so I took a walk with my "great Grecian nose and my lovely backside" and smelled the orange blossoms—those amazing, profuse clusters of small white bells so many of which fall victim to the wind or rains with only a few of those thousands bearing fruit—like ideas

I sometimes have but discard before they ripen or have a chance to see if they'll really bear fruit.

I also knew what Justina wanted.

I called her back. "What does it make you think of?" she asked.

"Oranges," I teased.

"Ah, you'll be sorry for that," she promised.

"Not oranges? What does it make you think of?"

"Sasha, I will never, never tell you now. You can tie me to the bedposts and threaten to have your way with me, promise to violate me with all sorts of lewd and lascivious acts, and I'll not tell you now. Never!"

I knew she was laughing, because we had both joked about the fact that there were no bedposts in motels to tie her to with her silk scarves, but we enjoyed every other "lewd and lascivious" act we could imagine. Only with Justina they became holy.

"Dearest One, tell me what it is you will never reveal. I can't live without knowing. Tell me all the details of the never-to-be-revealed secret. Now, Justina." I knew if I said her name exactly right she would give in.

She wanted a picnic at sundown when the scent of the orange blossoms was strongest. She hinted that soon after, it would be dark and lonely if we found the right spot. "I'll bring my mink coat—you know the one from the limo—and we can use it for a picnic blanket; then if it gets cold later, we can crawl under it."

She wasn't joking. Her black mink coat was a laugh. It was quintessential Justina. She absolutely adored the sensuality of the fur against her face and body, stuck her nose into the fur while she was wearing it to "smell its perfume" when really, it was all her own perfume, but why argue? For all that, she really did not value the coat for its monetary value. When she suggested using it for a picnic blanket, she meant it. When I reminded her of its cost, she scoffed, "But Sasha, it is only a thing! If I have to take care of it, it would lose all its allure—I don't want the responsibility of it as if it were my child. The whole point of luxuries is that they are for your enjoyment, not for caring for. It's not as if this is irreplaceable. And if it is gone, so what? I will always know the pleasures of it, and here in the desert, I don't think I have to worry about being cold. Furs aren't for warmth anyway, at least not in this desert."

It wasn't that she was irresponsible. She just had a different set of values from most people, had no use for acquiring things. What she did have was wealthy relatives, and she was the recipient of their cast-off antiques. But her favorite piece of furniture was what was probably an inexpensive piece to begin with—an oak chest she bought for $15 in a junk store. She had stripped it down to the bare wood, then stained it fire-engine red.

The mink was an almost-brand-new hand-me-down from her mother. Perhaps if she had bought and paid for the mink with her own money, she would have felt differently about it? "No. I wouldn't buy one—it's just so far away from anything I really care about. I have to tell you, Sasha, I do adore it in its own way, but I don't need it, do you see the difference? I can live without. That doesn't mean I don't appreciate having it... but never enough to have it discipline me."

It was my turn to laugh. I couldn't imagine anyone disciplining Justina, ever. When I think about her, I concentrate on these— what's the word?—irrepressible? wacky? qualities because they are so unknown to me. To the rest of the world she was a sensible, even unapproachable professional. I wondered if she found expression of that unused (or was it new) side of herself in our relationship and that was its core—the freedom to squander her suppressed person in those passionate moments? She was frightened, yet fearless; mysterious, yet honest; abandoned, but thoughtful and responsible, playful and serious. And I wondered so often what I would find in my depths when and if I found the freedom to let go. Just as often, I wondered what she found in me.

One early evening we had fallen asleep after our loving, and I awakened first. I watched her sleep for a while, and then as if she became aware of someone watching her, she awakened. "What?" she asked drowsily, moving even closer into the cradle of my arm. "What are you thinking?"

"I was wondering what you see in me—aside from the fact that I'm a great lover, of course..."

She raised one eyebrow at that and smiled, then was thoughtful, "You are my parent."

When I was visibly shocked at the implication of that, she laughed, then turned serious. "No, no, my darling. Never fear. I'm not that "keenky"—I mean my spiritual parent. You've given me the right to be myself which is like being born all over again. You tolerate my silliness—actually, you probably rather like it—and…" She paused and I waited. She sighed. "You know instinctively who I am. I don't have to invent myself for you nor hide from you. I think somehow you knew who and what I was when you sat in my classes. You probably didn't even know exactly what you knew then. But you set me free in this strange way, which is what being born is all about."

We lay there, our bodies warm and damp against each other, the perfume of them coupled with the scent of the linens (which she had sprayed with lavender mist when we arrived), each of us considering what she just said. Justina is for me the essence of freedom—in thought and action. Not that she is careless or uncaring with her freedom, but somehow she seems so eager to gather up every positive atom from life and return it back into the ether. I can't imagine her feeling restrained knowing her as I now do.

She turned so we were face to face, her arm folded under her head, "Sasha, I'm like a tree, you know?—sturdy and straight, rigid and strong and very unyielding until the winds catch at my leafy crown, blowing the anchored stems every which way. Then I don't know if my roots are mighty enough, deep enough to keep me grounded, or if I'll topple over and upset that soft underbelly of mine—that mossy blanket of sweet decay at my base which is needed for nourishment.

"And you, my love, are a zephyr—softly and quietly, and ever so slowly, blowing whispers through the leaves urging them to dance a ballet on their single-toed stems, changing my whole environment—the shadows on the trunk and even on the earth below—fresh air that enriches me much as a gentle rain might.

"But you are also a tornado assaulting me with a mighty force. Some leaves are blown into oblivion—I'll never see them again.

Others fall to the ground. But all those leaves you displace let in the sunlight and warmth. You have only to exhale and I tremble." And I thought, "You are like that for me, too." But unlike Justina, I have spent my life assaulted by the negative, and I identified much more with the storm and its confusion than with the sunlight and the warmth. So I said nothing, choosing instead to embrace her, to bury my nose in her neck, to draw her even closer to me.

CHAPTER ELEVEN

Graduation was finally here! The drill went like this. Someone reviewed our transcripts to see that we really qualified, and when that was official, we got the rest of the package: forms to fill out for our caps and gowns, invitations, directions, schedules, even an admonition to "comport" ourselves in a business-like manner during the ceremony. Whoa! We knew what that meant—no funny stuff—no balloons, bubbles, silliness.

I awoke that morning feeling like I always do when I am going to see Justina—and even though we had talked about not making any kind of contact with each other, just seeing her, knowing she was there, was enough to make me feel good—exalted. And of course, it was this long-awaited day. I could hardly believe that more than three years had gone by since I made the decision to go back to school, spurred on, I have to admit, by the fact that my company was paying all the tuition—and it was a big chunk of change at this private school.

So I considered whether they had gotten a bargain or not while I was shaving. I knew, in spite of all the hard work, the hours when I would rather have been doing something else, I was very grateful for the opportunity. Not everyone in our class felt that way. Some were still in the same jobs they had when they started, and I could see why. A degree in anything wasn't going to change their attitudes or their work ethic. And their expectations that this degree was some kind of magic were dashed, making them even more disillusioned.

But many of us had seen rewards, and I was certainly one of those. Earlier in the year I was promoted to this job—just before our first research class. And I interviewed just last week with the plant manager himself for a more prestigious promotion—my own office instead of sharing one with my manager and two others. If I get the job, it will entail some travel eventually—technical support and customer service with our plants around the country; more mental and people stuff than production. None of this would have happened without my going for that degree, and certainly the job interview I just had would not have happened without my research project. We'll see...

But today is graduation day, and I am preparing myself for that special moment when I have to climb the steps to the stage alone to receive the Paul Bowers Award. I'm hoping all I have to do is say, "Thank you. I appreciate this very much." And I'll be saying that silently to Justina as well. I'll never know how much my wanting to impress her influenced the kind of job I did with that, but I do know I have to factor it in.

The happy confusion in the auditorium anterooms was infectious. After I found seats for Anna and the kids and my granny, I went to the designated area for our group. It was like New Year's Eve with everyone high-fiving everyone else, wishing each other big salary increases. It was general but civilized bedlam. We remembered we had been warned about our "comportment." We had our gowns on, and everyone was asking which side of the mortarboard the tassels hung from. The women were complaining about the caps ruining their hair and running to the ladies' room to see how they looked. The guys could have cared less. We all just wanted to get it over with and get on to the after-graduation parties.

Finally, someone called us all to order, and Kate Milligrew, the VP and Justina's friend, gave us our last minute instructions. We were to assemble with our classmates, write our names on the cards being distributed. "Legibly. You all know what that means? So that even a fool can read them. And if you have a name that might be difficult to pronounce, write it out phonetically." Of course I thought of Justina... "When you ascend the stairs, you will hand your name to the person waiting there. Pause until your name is announced, then move to center stage where Dr. Morrison will be waiting to shake your hand and congratulate you. He will shake your right hand as he offers you a paper roll tied in ribbon with his left. Take it with your left hand and say, 'Thank you.' Then walk across the stage, down the other side and back to your seat. This is a ceremony. Your actual degrees will be mailed to you next week. Any questions?"

No one had any.

Then, "Alexander Psipsopoulos. Where are you?" I raised my hand.

She walked over to where I stood. "Please make sure that you have an aisle seat, so that when your name is called to receive the Paul Bowers Award, you are free to go up and receive it without struggling across your classmates."

And that is how my classmates learned that I was to receive this award. I shrugged off the congratulations, said I was as surprised as anyone when I heard about it. All that conversation was cut short when we heard the music change from a string quartet in the background to "Pomp and Circumstance."

We lined up and started to move forward. The faculty formed two lines in the lobby through which we marched, applauding us as we entered the auditorium from the back. I saw Justina among them, shaking hands with the students who broke rank to hug her and other faculty. I was not one of them. I saw at a glance that she was fighting tears. And more than anyone there, I wanted to touch her, even momentarily, but we had made this promise to each other. So we avoided looking at each other—even that would have been too much with all this emotion.

We were all seated when the faculty march began, the students applauding the faculty now. And there she was, her confident strides in time with the music in her doctoral hood, and that crazy hat that looked like a pleated beret, her colleague in similar regalia. It wasn't quite like the first time I saw her, but this was the woman I made love to—naked—in all her professorial garb. The irony was not lost on me.

The program began with the presentation of the flags, then the convocation, benediction, and the speeches. And then, lost as I was in the ceremony, I suddenly heard the words, "Paul Bowers Award," and I was aware that this was it!

Dr. Morrison introduced Paul Bowers and each of them took a turn at reviewing the research project process and my selection. Bowers read a few lines from the plant manager's letter to the selection committee—the part about my work saving my department and the company over $100,000 this year alone.

At the right moment, I got up, went to the stage to receive the award, tried not to mumble my thanks and was about to leave, when the president of the university said, "Stay right here a moment, Alexander. We have another person to honor with the Faculty of the Year Award—someone you know very well." My knees began to shake, I swear they did. Why no one noticed and came forward to give me a chair I'll never know. But I stayed. What choice did I have?

Dr. Morrison droned on about the annual faculty award, voted by students, how the faculty were the heart of the university, and gave a short version of Justina's resumé, her time with the university. I was paralyzed. I couldn't see, but I was aware of some movement among the faculty, and suddenly, she was standing alongside me, thanking Dr. Morrison, saying something about how students deserve the awards and faculty are just there to guide them. Then she moved directly in front of me, offered that hand that in other circumstances traveled all over my body, and congratulated me, in that business voice of hers. I think I thanked her for putting up with me in class, and the students all laughed. And then, thankfully, we were free to leave. We left the stage together in spite of our promises. I went down the stairs first and turned back to take her hand as she descended. Her hand was shaking, and now the tears were spilling quietly down her cheeks.

I was in a daze. When our row rose to march towards our degrees, I followed everyone else like a robot. I gave my name card to the proper person, walked once again halfway across the stage, and Dr. Morrison congratulated me again for my fine work. I walked across the other half, following the person in front of me. It was too much. I was overcome. Happily, there were a few hundred more students whose names still had to be called, and I settled down somewhat.

We marched out of the auditorium to the recessional; administration and faculty first, then the students, past our families who were seated behind us, and I saw my granny, wiping her eyes, seated next to Anna and the children. And I suddenly felt very American.

CHAPTER TWELVE

When I added my small stack of clothes to the pile Justina had created in the tiny trunk of her car, it made a pyramid. She raised her eyebrows. "Ah, you travel light," she smiled. "But no worry, you won't need much." I had no way of knowing all that she had managed to pack into that small space. Finding out later was a revelation.

It was Friday afternoon, and we were on our way to the mountains for an entire weekend. I had promised to design a complicated, computerized sound system for the mountaintop retreat of a wealthy Greek friend. Perhaps he was a distant relative—who knew? It is difficult to keep track of all the family ties, especially in this country where, if you are a recent immigrant, you are automatically considered "family" in the small but thriving Greek community in this city.

My kids had things they were unwilling to give up to come to the mountains: one, a birthday party of a friend; the other, a Pop Warner football game. Anna said if this was more important than being with them, I might just as well go alone.

It was the chance Justina and I had been looking for—a way to get away together with the least amount of deceit. My friends, whose house it was, had gone to Chicago on business, so there was no chance he or his wife would appear. We were as safe from the view of other humans as we could ever be.

Justina was in a state of unprecedented joy! Finally, no watching the clock. "At least until Sunday," she said. "And we can celebrate your birthday. I'll give you a surprise party."

"What kind of surprise? Who will you invite?" I was tentative.

"Only the two of us—isn't that enough for a party? The surprise you will have to wait for."

So, in spite of my reluctance to plan for such things, here we were taking off in her silly car with the top down and the heat on. It was Fall, her favorite time of the year, and she wanted "to feel it all around me—the wind, the smell, the colors, the special silence of Autumn. We can put the top up later, when it's too cold to bear." Her mink coat was stuffed rather unceremoniously in the space behind the seats, and we added my jacket to that assortment of things we were carrying there.

The drive on the Interstate took about an hour and a half. Justina drove, so we cut fifteen minutes off that time. She loved her car for its power and speed, and she used it. Often she drove up the Interstate just for relaxation, her music playing. She would get to a lookout, and if it was isolated enough, spend time meditating, climb back in and drive home, refreshed.

After leaving the Interstate, we had another hour's drive to reach the house. We made it just as the sun was setting. It was the beginning of a weekend I will never forget.

I couldn't believe the things we unloaded from her car: hanging bags of clothes ("But we're in the mountains, Justina." "Darling, we are still civilized…"), her inevitable picnic hamper which we'd surely use, other boxes of food packed in dry ice. True to form, she had planned for a week when all we had was a weekend. She was always consistent…

The house was a kind of glass igloo, a geodesic dome constructed of glass triangles, perched high on a crest, yet set snugly into the mountain with a spectacular 360-degree view of the area. I knew it would be just the kind of place Justina would adore, and I was excited to be bringing her to this remote, romantic spot.

She was more impressed than I had ever seen her. "It's not just a mountaintop retreat; it's an aerie… it's a contemporary hogan. Oh, Sasha," as she moved from place to place. "What exquisite taste. It's so elegant and simple. Surely, the people who built this are artists? The colors, the perfect choices… I don't ever want to leave. Oh, thank you, thank you, for bringing me here." This, as she threw her arms around me, then danced off to see something else. We were in a single, enormous room, open to the sky and the world.

I stood and watched her as I could from the center of this house, her unbridled joy infecting me. She stood at different windows, looking out, then looking back into the interior and out the other sides, savoring each for its special perspective and vista. All of the necessities were luxuriously here. No walls inhibited the view from any spot. The bathroom, an apartment-sized room, was on the lower floor with its own fabulous appointments including a small fireplace built into the wall, a Jacuzzi, and exercise equipment, as well as an adjoining dressing room. There were three glass walls to the world (who but the birds and wild animals could see us?) that followed the angle of the mountainside into which it was built, so that it was almost invisible. Its roof created a deck for the upstairs which reached out over the edge of the land, and it was from here that we watched the sun set.

There was a huge circular fireplace, slightly elevated, in the center of the room, with its own glass walls so that the fire could be enjoyed from any place in the house. A slim flue rose and exited through the center of the roof. The exterior wall of the flue was constructed of some new hi-tech metal alloy that had the look of glass and which reflected the light from the windows so that even the flue seemed not to interfere with the space. Justina was thoughtful for a moment, staring into a place of her own. "I am reminded of a great honor I once had," she said quietly.

"When I worked on the Indian reservation, I had a very good friend whose daughter lived in a traditional hogan on the Navajo reservation. Since Anglos are not considered to be tuned into traditional Indian ways, they are rarely invited to participate in family events unless they are trusted.

"My friend invited me to spend the weekend with her at her daughter's." She was quiet and still. "It was a religious experience for me. Indian reservations always have that effect on me anyway, but here we were in this remote place.

"We arrived in the dark, so I didn't have my bearings. In the morning, it was like this—silent and remote—except we were in the valley and the red, rocky mountains rose up around us. There was not another dwelling or anything else human to be seen. It was other worldly—unlike anything I had ever experienced. I was greatly moved.

"That was a different kind of simplicity—the simplicity of living with the earth. Like this, there was a fire spot in the center, but it was an earthen floor. No flue, merely a smoke hole in the center of the hogan roof."

We were standing at the windows looking out into the dusk, arms around each other's waists.

"When I awakened the second morning, there was a gentle fire still warming us. As I lay on my pallet, I watched snow flakes filter down that smoke hole and disappear as the heat from the fire rose up. I don't know why that was such an emotional scene for me. No one else was yet awake, so I lay in my own space and time and quiet, almost afraid to move, to alter the beauty before me.

"Understand, from the viewpoint of most Anglos, this was a mean, poverty-stricken hovel—dirt floors, no electricity, kerosene or some kind of oil lamps, cooking over that same fire that warmed us. But I was transported and so grateful to be there. Never will an honor mean more to me than for that family to have welcomed me into their lives and their home. I never see snow, nor think of it, that that vision does not play in my head and the emotion it evoked then is recalled with all its majesty. And I am feeling that same thing here, with all the affluence and luxury. It is a different kind of simplicity, but these people understand."

She tried to lighten the moment. "Their bathroom, too, didn't intrude into their living space." And she laughed softly. "The other vision I can recall with exquisite precision is the picture of my footsteps in the snow. Since I was the first awake, I had the good fortune to make a path to the outhouse."

"Now that I would like to have seen—especially you in your silk nightie on the way to the outhouse…"

She smiled at the memory, and I thought, "Will this woman never cease to amaze me with her experiences? Who would ever put Justina Packard in a hogan with an outhouse? And who would believe her—that it was the kind of emotional experience she described?"

As if reading my thoughts, she continued. "I know. You just don't see me there, do you? People who get to know me tell me that all the time. Once I went to some other mountains with a friend—we were going to occupy a broken-down ranch house for the weekend, and we were chopping wood for the fire. Suddenly, she stopped and sat down, laying her ax on the ground, roaring with laughter. When I asked her what was so funny, she said, 'No one who knows you casually or professionally would ever believe the sight of you chopping wood. Me? Yes. Everyone knows I grew up on a ranch. But you? With your hats and gloves and elegance? Never. I could verify it and swear to it, but no one would buy it. It's just too funny, too outrageous to consider, but here you are in your jeans throwing an ax around. I think I'll just kick back and enjoy it. It's one of those rare moments in life.' And she let me finish the job." She was quiet, remembering...

"Funny thing is, I like chopping wood simply because it is an unexpected ability. I want to know everything—how to do everything. I won't get another chance, I think, so I want to do everything I can while I'm here."

Again, shifting moods, she moved into the circle of my arms. "Thank you, Sasha, for this—for everything; mostly for me, selfish, greedy thing that I am. Hold me..." And a few moments later, "Hold on to me, okay?"

I had always appreciated this house before, but with the children, I was always watching, afraid they would wreck something, even though they spent most of the time outdoors. With Justina, I looked through her eyes and saw levels of care and planning I had never seen before, and I realized that so often she was like a pair of wonderful magic glasses I could put on and look out at a world I wouldn't see without her.

She was right about the owners—they were artists, although not professionals. They were honest, hard-working business people with the senses of the ancient Greeks who appreciated and were able to recreate timelessness, to create a beautiful space that was as she said, "Music. That's what it makes me think of—music: the ideal blend of harmonics…mathematics…to touch the soul. How wonderful, Sasha. Do you really know what joy it is for me to be here? I couldn't create this, but I appreciate every detail they included, and more especially everything they left out.

"Put the sound system in the bathroom or underground. Don't violate a thing here. It is almost as if our presence here is too much, do you know what I mean? As if we were intruding on perfect space—the gods watching must annoyed that we've added ourselves to it—we are too much. It's a good thing I cherish your beautiful presence or I would ask you to go. I can't see myself taking up any of the space, so my own presence doesn't violate my vision. And yours is always such a joy, I can hardly fault you. I couldn't stand being here with anyone else. Thank you.

"I'll stop as soon as I get used to it. I know how you hate my excesses. It's just such a surprise, I'm stunned."

She was still standing in the circle of my arms, but she moved suddenly. "We have to put all the stuff away. Let's hurry and get that done so we can just be us. It's cold enough for a fire, yes? If you do that, I'll take care of the kitchen…Where shall I put our things? Where do we sleep—make love?"

I hit a button on one of the long couches and it whirred a bit, unfolding itself, and turned into a king-sized bed. Instantly, her face clouded.

"What?" I quickly asked.

"Sasha, I can't sleep there in that bed with you…"

"Why? For goodness sake, why not?" Now I was puzzled. What had happened?

Quietly, insidiously, our other lives came to join our party. "I just couldn't. I'm sorry. I know you've come up here with Anna and the children. I couldn't possibly sleep in that bed with you knowing you had slept in it with her. I just didn't think that far ahead when we planned this. I'm sorry." And she turned abruptly toward the kitchen.

I stopped her from going—put my hand into hers. "Justina, we don't have to sleep on that bed. There are other beds. All the couches turn into beds. We'll choose another. It's all right."

But she walked away and busied herself inside the refrigerator putting her collection of foods away, stacking the empty boxes off to one side. She was quiet. Then, "I just didn't even consider that. I'm sorry. I know we've loved each other on any number of anonymous beds in motels, and I know the bed shouldn't be important. But this, I can't do it."

"Look, Justina, if I told you I have never had sex with Anna on that bed, would that help? You know we've only ever been up here with the kids sleeping in this same room. You can see that although there are many couches that turn into beds, this house was really designed for only two wanting privacy."

"No. It wouldn't change anything. Look, Sasha, go get the wood, okay, Dear? I'll get control of myself in a few minutes. I think I have to deal with this alone." And when I stood there, feeling overwhelmed and helpless, she attempted a weak smile. "Take the empty boxes with when you go, okay?"

So I took the empty boxes and went out for the wood. I stood for a while gazing at the sky which was to me as mysterious as this woman. She knew I would never divorce Anna. It was never even a matter of discussion. She said she could never live with me, "Stubborn mule that you are." She said what we had was something else. And then just when I was beginning to think I understood her, this.

When I returned, she was gone. I found her sitting out on the deck, on the floor leaning against one of the uprights, her eyes fixed on that same sky I had just sought answers from. She was smoking a cigarette. I knew she carried an unopened package of cigarettes with her at all times, although she was not a smoker. "When I am agitated, I can blow away some of my anxious energy with the smoke. And since no one can smoke around anyone else any more, it is always a few moments of private time, when I can analyze my distress…"

I sat down alongside her and took her hand. And we sat there lost in the vastness of the universe, the clouds, a lighter shade than the sky, sliding slowly across the half moon and the stars, and the luminescent stars—were they shedding tears or laughing at us when their light sparkled and faded? I wanted to make it right for her so she could recapture her earlier pleasure, but I was at a loss how to do it. So I waited.

She was remote and quiet for what seemed a long time, especially for Justina. After a bit, I could feel her relax, and she laid her head on my chest. "It's freezing out here. Did you make the fire?" And she looked up at me.

"No. When I came back in and you were gone, I only wanted to find you, to comfort you if I could. Are you all right?"

"Yes. I'm truly sorry, my love. I was unprepared for that. I just didn't think about it when we planned to come here. If I had, I would have dealt with it already. It's just that the way I love you always seems so pure to me. I know that's stupid under the circumstances. I know you have sex with Anna, but I don't really want to know it. I just couldn't possibly ever love you in her bed. It's somehow unclean." As I breathed in to respond, she added, "No, I don't mean in the sense of cleanliness, like dirt, but the thought of it violates me in some profound way."

I tried a light touch. "Look, Justina, we'll go out in your car and start all over again, okay? We can fumble and grope with the console between us…"

She smiled bravely. "No it's going to be too cold tonight. But could we sleep on the floor? Would you mind?"

"Justina, we can sleep anywhere you want. But I assure you we can use one of the other beds that the kids usually sleep in."

"No, that's just as bad. I don't want to be thinking about the other people you belong to when we are together. It's just that one's own bed is such a personal space, do you know what I mean? It's as much out of respect for Anna as it is for me. I know that must sound bizarre to you, but I can't help it; it's how I feel and how I am. I have a real sense of privacy, and somehow I don't want her to sleep in a place where we've been together either. We have so little that's just absolutely our very own, I want to treasure it and keep it sacred." She had brought out an ashtray for her cigarette which she had already finished, and she moved to pick it up, then turned, "This will pass, and I'll be all right soon, I promise. I just have to regain my perspective."

I did not let go of her hand, and we sat a while longer, neither of us daring, I think, to make the wrong move, waiting for the mood to pass. "Can I get you a glass of wine? I turned the hot water on as soon as we arrived; it should be warm in the Jacuzzi…"

She smiled. "Do I have to choose between the Jacuzzi and the fire?"

"No, my love, we can satisfy your desire for excess. I'll build a small fire down there and we can take our supper down. In the meantime, I'll get the fire going up here, so it's warm when we get back upstairs."

We got up then and went indoors. She looked back over her shoulder. "Are you hungry?"

I moved alongside her and touched her lips with my finger. "For you…"

She smiled. "We can't take all that food back, and you know it's a 'sin' to throw it out. I'll make a tray of munchies and we can graze with our wine. I'll do the food if you do the fires."

So we made two trips downstairs before we actually got into the hot tub. Justina could take a head of leafy lettuce and make a tray full of food that was a still-life fit for a museum. This one had cold Polish sausage, barbecued chicken strips, cheese, marinated vegetables and fresh berries sprinkled all over. We got into the hot tub with our wine glasses, the bottle on a ledge, and soaked away her angst. It seems neither of us was hungry for food; it was still there in the morning, and she had forgotten to worry about wasting food.

She found blankets and quilts and extra pillows stashed away in a linen closet off the bathroom and took them upstairs to make our bed. She had put on a satin nightgown and robe the color of the white wine we had been drinking and went diligently about the business of creating a bed for us near the fireplace. I noticed that she selected a spot as far away from the hated bed as she could and still take advantage of the fire, and I smiled sadly.

As we lay in this bed she had made, her early words to me, "Very fragile," passed through my mind briefly before more sensual thoughts emerged. Perhaps it was that recognition of her fragility that created this ethereal atmosphere in which we loved each other that night. I can't quite identify what it was, but it was different from any other time we had been together—and it wasn't just me, I could feel it in her, too—this other-worldly, eternal aura which encapsulated us, made us newly quiet as if even our own sounds would destroy our solitude.

We had never spent a whole night together, and just before she fell asleep, she said, sleepily, "Sasha, I have a confession to make."

"Um?"

"I snore sometimes. Just nudge me and I'll turn over and stop."

I laughed quietly as I, too, dozed off. Justina snore? I loved it. I'd have something to tease her about forever.

I'll never know if she snored. We slept soundly. Once during the night I awakened and tried to remember why I was sleeping on the floor. I moved to see if she was covered and she crawled over in her sleep to fit herself into me. Her naked body lay curled into mine. She was warm, and the scent of her joined with the scent of our loving, a reminder of our earlier passion. I could feel myself wanting her again, an urge quickly replaced by a sweet tenderness. I wanted to protect her, to keep her from harm, safe from the world for which she pretended to be so well equipped, but from which, I had grown to know, she had few defenses. Only the circumstances of her life, orchestrated by some kind gods who watched over her, had kept her free from harm up till now. I put my arm gently around her so as not to waken her.

CHAPTER THIRTEEN

I woke to the smell of coffee. She must have set the timer last night while fixing her tray of munchies. She was still tucked into my side, one arm under her pillow and the other thrown over me. As if conscious of my waking, she murmured, "I love you, Sasha. Good morning, my love."

The fire had dwindled and it was chilly. The coffee smelled inviting, but Justina smelled even more inviting. She uncurled herself and stretched, then looked at me innocently, "I don't know what you like for breakfast."

Memories of the night, the smell of her, moved me. If I knew anything at all about this woman, it was that she hated getting out of bed in the morning. She had said so often enough. "Are you ready to get up?" I asked.

"I never want to get up. Can we spend the entire weekend here?"

And so we awakened as we had gone to sleep, lost in the caresses and the pleasures we always found in each other—this, our first morning waking up together—different from last night. Breakfast and the coffee were not on our agenda that early morning.

She said later in the morning that she had some things to do to prepare for the party, and I went to look at the proposed sound system. After listening to Justina the night before, I realized any equipment on the main level was out, so I searched around for space on the lower level and found it in the dressing room. The system was programmable for twenty-four hours, so a single visit on any day was all that would be needed with no inconvenience.

We went for a walk after lunch. It was crisp as only an Autumn day in the mountains can be, yet it was warm in the sun. Justina picked some feathery silver stems and colored leaves to take back. We loved each other out there on the mountaintop. She was her usual abandoned self; her misgivings about the bed and my family seemed similarly abandoned here where the earth was our bed and we were alone together.

I was reminded of my dream which I still had not recounted to Justina, but I didn't want to introduce any sadness into our afternoon. I knew she would understand the significance of those chains and it would pain her. But that afternoon, I felt as free as if I had soared away from the mountain top with her in my dream, as if I had finally released myself from those chains—inhaling that raw forest commingling of pines and damp soil, feeling both the sun and Justina's warmth infuse me as we coupled there under the sky. I briefly wondered if it was possible to become innocent and pure after one had already shook hands with cynicism and wariness? If it was possible, I felt ready that afternoon to walk that path of resurrection.

We were once again soaking in the tub when she asked, "Did I tell you the party begins with cocktails at five, dinner at seven?" And she turned coy. "I've not planned anything after dinner…" She turned my wrist to see what time it was. "It will take me just a few minutes to organize everything but a while to dress, and I still have to set the table."

She slid down so that her chin was resting on the water, then she looked over at me and turned serious. "Sasha, anything I could think of that I wanted to buy for your birthday would be so showy, so magnificent, so expensive it would be hard to explain…"

"Justina, you shower me with your gifts every day. Every day is my birthday with you. Please…" I was embarrassed. No one ever made a big deal out of my birthday. To be honest, so often I just plain didn't know how to react to the gift that Justina was, let alone to acknowledge that or any of her gifts.

"Well, I have to say it. There is nothing I could ever buy you that would reflect what you mean to me, and faced with that, I decided to give you a memory, a special evening instead."

My embarrassment faded, and I was sincere. The memory of the afternoon and the emotion it evoked returned. "Sweetie, every time I am with you it is special; it could not be otherwise. You have given me memories that will last my life, things no one could purchase, moments and hours that no one else could give. It is more than I ever expected to have." It was as close as I could come to telling her how I felt about her.

She leaned over and kissed me. "Well then, let's go get ready for the party. If you do the fire, I'll set the table, then we can dress. Deal?"

She put on a silk shirt that didn't quite reach her knees, a pair of sheer black panty hose, and we went upstairs to get the party under way. And I put on a robe that was hanging on a hook in the dressing room.

Upstairs, from the jumble of her baggage, she produced a table set for royalty. Us. She had brought china with cobalt blue rims set in silver frames, matching cobalt colored stemware. There was a bowl she started to fiddle with. In the center were the wild stems and leaves she had brought back from our walk and long, cobalt blue, pencil-thin candles protruding from the arrangement. It seemed there were dozens of them... Against the silvery feathers of her wild stems and gold and red leaves, she had created an arrangement that was about two-feet wide. "Low," she said, as I knelt before the fireplace urging the flames on, and she stepped back from it to view her handiwork. "It has to be low so I can see you across the table."

She put some things in the oven, set the timer, looked at the clock, and said, "We have an hour to dress. Enough time?"

"An hour?" I wondered. What would take an hour? My thoughts raced to some other way to spend the time but, "Yes, it will take me that long. And maybe you, too. Want to shower with—or alone?"

"With."

"Let's go." She paused at the top of the staircase to the bathroom, looked once more at the table with approval, and we went down to get ready for my birthday party.

Showering with Justina was always erotic. It was foreplay with all the sensuality and sexuality one could conjure up. It wasn't just soap—it was soap that evoked spring flowers and rain. It wasn't just a rub down—it was a slow dance of her hands all over my body. It wasn't warm water raining down over me, it was a purification of the soul—baptism, absolution. It was a ritual. And it held all the healing qualities and promise of such a ritual.

Then watching Justina dress was a revelation all its own. It was like the first time I saw her in class with her stacks of papers and transparencies. Only now it was beautiful bottles and tubes. She was trying to keep her things contained, not to make a mess, but she was so concentrated on what she was doing, the resources she used were incidental to the job at hand. She would have said, "Things," if I had asked.

Finally, she was done with her hair and her make-up. I had nothing to do but watch, sitting there in my borrowed robe. I was not bored but fascinated. She didn't mind my watching, blew kisses to me when she remembered I was there. Now she changed into the robe from the night before, nothing else.

Then, finally, "Okay, let's do it."

She took down a white nylon bag and draped it over her arm. "Your clothes, my love, are in the black nylon bag. I don't want you to see me until I'm dressed, and I don't want to see you either. I'll finish upstairs. You can come calling for me when you're ready." And she dropped that white nylon bag on the floor for a moment and took one last bottle from the table—not just any bottle, but a crystal atomizer with a black silken hose at the end of which was a black meshy bladder and aimed it at her neck, her wrists, her crotch, behind her knees. No wonder she always smelled so delicious!

She took from the closet a long, black nylon bag, said, "This one's yours," kissed me lightly and went up the stairs.

Now what? I unzipped the bag. In it was a black tuxedo with a pleated dress shirt. In the bottom were black patent leather shoes with white silk socks stuffed inside. I laughed out loud at the sight of those white socks. I wondered how it would all fit, but I should have had more trust. I had only worn a tuxedo when I was married and when I was best man at my brother's wedding (when we had worn the traditional black socks). Tucked into the pocket of the tuxedo was a pair of black silk bikini undershorts. Right down to the last detail.

I dressed alone, without her, but consumed with thoughts of her and surrounded by her scent which she had left behind. If I had selected and tried these things on, I would have chosen them for myself. Everything fit perfectly. How did she do these things?

Had I given her enough time to finish? Should I wait? I looked at the watch she hated. It was three minutes before five. I'd wait the three minutes.

But from above, I heard music, and I knew she was ready.

I went up after one last glance in the mirrors. If I was ever going to be elegant, this was my day. I suddenly remembered there were no mirrors upstairs for that last glance for her. I was feeling self-conscious, but ready for whatever she had planned.

She was standing, across the room from the staircase, waiting for me, her back to the windows. She was dressed in a white strapless gown with a wide black satin belt that echoed my own black satin cummerbund; hers was beaded in an intricate pattern. It was her only adornment; no jewelry, no earrings. Her shoulders were bare, but huge sleeves covered her upper arms. The skirt was shorter in front and curved upward toward that secret place where her legs ended, and the back swept the floor. It was simple but spectacular. We stood for a moment, looking at each other across the room, then moved at the same time toward each other.

"Happy birthday, Darling Sasha; happy, happy birthday," and she was pressed against my chest, encircled by my arms, kissing me with gentle, whispery kisses all over my face. She stood back. "Now. Let me really look at you, so I can photograph you in my mind, so I can always remember."

The last of the sun radiated behind me; Justina glowed in front of me. My birthday was not for ten days, but it was a moment to be born and to die for.

The cobalt blue stemmed glasses sat on a coffee table. "Will you open the wine? Since we never eat, I didn't make masses of food. There's escargot and crusty bread to go with our drinks. Enough, I think."

We watched the sun disappear, then the shading of the half light, and finally the darkness from the night before. She lit a set of candles on the coffee table and we had the light from the fire. We could sniff whatever was cooking in the oven, but it wasn't ready yet.

"Tell me about other birthdays." So we exchanged our favorite birthday stories and even spoke of the disappointing ones as we sipped our wine. She was turned toward me on the couch, her shoes slipped off now, and her knees tucked up under her as I remembered her from that first time we were together.

"It's going to take a long time to get you undressed. We'd better see about dinner." And she was off to the kitchen.

It didn't matter what we ate, it was beautiful. Chicken Kiev ("A family recipe from my real homeland…") with a creamy mushroom sauce, contrasted against the blue of the plate rim. I remember the visions rather than the tastes. All the while I ate, I was tasting her, savoring her, tuning into the other senses that she provoked. The food was almost an intrusion—as we had always found it to be. I wanted to sit back and through that bouquet of candles, the candlelight, stare at the woman who had given me the gift of this evening.

The soft, slow music continued. "Adagios, all of them," she said when I asked. "From Albinoni, Barber, and de Boisvallee through Khachaturian and Marcello and on to Schumann. Actually, I cheated a bit and put some Tchaikovsky in—some ballet music, 'Romeo and Juliet,' which seemed appropriate," and she looked up questioningly; then continued, "A matter of my homeland… I just re-taped them so they would be continuous.

"In alphabetical order?" I teased.

"No, I'm not that compulsive. As I found them among the other tapes and CDs. Was it a good choice?"

"Yes, you know how I appreciate the slow, the sensual. The best choice."

After dinner she fixed two sambucas, and we took the flaming glasses back to the couch. We watched the pale blue flames in our darker blue glasses; hypnotized, prolonging the moment. Then we clapped our hands over the flame to extinguish it and wished each other the traditional health, wealth, and happiness that the three coffee beans represented. I had moved to be close to her, our bodies touching; she was soft, supple, pliant... mine.

We sipped the sweet, syrupy, fiery liqueur, and I was reminded of the sweet, syrupy, fiery liqueurs which she could produce in both of us.

She was right. It took a long time for her to undress me. She paused to count my shirt studs every time she took one out. "We don't want to lose any of them," she teased. It was not so with her. One zip down her back and she was naked except for her black panty hose. But they can take a long time to get off if you are careful, and I was very careful.

There are those amorphous moments when Justina and I are together—and I am totally absorbed by our loving—her flesh, our eagerness, and the thrill of our sexuality—when a fugitive, ephemeral nobility engulfs me, rises up from some unknown center of my being. It is elusive and fleeting and more than desire—drowned in the certain urgency of our desire—gone before I can grasp it, hold on to it. That night amid the tenderness and passion—our two bodies made one in the rapture of the moment, I thought I recognized it. Eternity.

We fell asleep where we lay—cocooned in this invisible, gossamer mesh that was even more compelling than sex. Justina did not care about making the bed this evening. She did not remind me that she snored, and I did not think about it. When I woke the next morning, we were lying under her mink coat, tightly wrapped around each other. She had gotten up sometime during the night and found the first thing she could to keep us warm beyond what we needed from each other.

When she woke, she said, "It's like going to church—being here with you on Sunday morning. Good morning, holy one."

"No, you are the holey one," I teased. We played for a while, made love, rested, and finally got up.

It was still early. We ignored the beautiful clothes strewn all over, the dirty dishes. "Later—we can do our chores later. Let's go walking." So we left it all behind and went tramping once again through the woods. We came to the spot where we had loved each other the day before and paused.

"Justina, thank you. It is the birthday that will remain for all time with me; better than any I ever had, had a right to expect. It can never be better. I want you to know that."

"I'm glad. But there's always next year…"

"No. It will never be better. Now I know exactly what you can do when you want to. You may be able to exceed yourself, but this had the element of complete surprise. I'm not sure I'll ever be surprised by you again. How did you know my sizes?"

"Well, I went to the tuxedo place and I lay on the floor and spread my legs and I said, 'He fits me here. His waist is here when he is on top of me. His arms end here when he holds me.' And they just took out their tapes and measured away. I deliberately went to one of those incredibly snooty places where they wouldn't register any kind of emotion—probably don't even know how to laugh. I did tell them to make sure the pants were pleated so there would be room for all of you for the whole night. They didn't need every measurement to be exact, you see, and which one should I have given in any event? This man never blinked an eye."

I knew she was putting me on, but I was still curious…

She laughed wickedly. "Darling, how many times have I undressed you? It is easy to see the labels in your shirt, to calculate your waist around which my own arms go so often. Your jeans label proclaims your pants length and waist for anyone to see anyway. It's just a bit of Sherlocking if you really want to know. I was most worried about the shoes, but I knew we wouldn't be dressed for long, and anyway you could take them off and display your beloved white socks if they were uncomfortable, as you could anything else that didn't fit. After all, it was to be your party…"

We did go back and do the chores. She was compulsive about leaving everything as we had found it: laundering the linens we had used, washing the robe. And then she was done and eager to stow our stuff and just sit and enjoy our last hours together in the house she appreciated so much. No extra "things."

We replayed the music from last night, both the tapes and the loving, but this time there was that quality of sadness, of goodbye. Even the music seemed more melancholy than slow and sensual. When I said that, she said, "That's how adagios are for me, too. They take on my mood. Maybe that's why I like them. They adapt to me instead of my having to adapt to them."

We had to leave finally. At the door she paused. "Goodbye wonderful place of love and beauty. Your space will always echo with our love, and so we leave that gift behind, invisible, thankfully, so as not to disturb the senses. And the love we gave each other here we will take away with us and cherish always, so you, glass hogan that you are, will be a part of us forever, too."

I wondered fleetingly how I could ever come back here with Anna and the children, and not weep for this time with Justina, but even as I thought it, I knew it would not be the same place to which I returned—this place I came to this time, this new place, this place where I had never been before.

CHAPTER FOURTEEN

It rained the night before Justina left—all night long—as I slept fitfully, thinking about her, with this other woman, my wife, asleep on the other side of the bed. It was as if we were casual travelers on a tour who had come to a hostel separately late at night, and there was only this one bed left. We were polite, said good night to each other, and each occupied our half, careful not to invade the other's space. The only way we could have been more isolated from each other in this bed would have been to climb into individual sleeping bags.

And so I thought of Justina. It was not unusual for me to lie here, like this, feeling her warmth, knowing her touch, wanting to be with her, anticipating the next time; only this night I knew the next time, if it was ever to be, would be long into the future.

Justina, who even in her sleep, searches for me, winds her legs around mine, maneuvers her body into mine until we are one… Justina, who makes me laugh when the last thing I feel like doing is laughing…Justina, who makes me angry with her avant-garde ideas, but makes me think… Justina, with her fairy dust and her picnic hamper full of useful but unused playthings…Justina, who loves me…

And so it has come to this—this woman who loves me is moving across the country and while she was here, I could not—would not?—say those words she wanted to hear. Not that she ever asked, but I knew. What I don't know is why I am such a donkey—why, until I knew she was leaving, I could not give her that pleasure.

For I do love her!

I have learned from her, finally, how to be generous and free with my emotion for her. It was her purple envelopes and the messages she tucked inside them that inspired me. I wrote her a letter after our last time together, and I've mailed it already so it will be waiting at her new apartment to assure her that this is not good-bye. For me to put my feelings into words and send them to her is an accomplishment. I could not have done this a year ago. So in spite of the fact that she probably thinks I am no more open now than I was when I met her, I know I have changed.

This day she is leaving here and beginning a new life—is the one year anniversary of our first night in her silly car, that car she is going to drive back East on her next trip. She will be more amazed than she was by the glass house when she gets to her new one. And my surprise is so contrary to anything she expects from me that I am sorry I won't be there to share her delight and bask in her pleasure; I know just how she will react, and I want so much to watch her joy—bask in the glow of her.

That twelve-page letter, in its passionate purple envelope, mailed to the florist, will be delivered with 365 roses—as many colors as the florist could find—will be waiting in her apartment when she arrives, one for every day of our loving so far. It starts out, "Beloved Justina," and ends with "For a good time, call Sasha. I'm at the same number where I've always been." She will smile among her tears at that little bit of humor and the irreverence she cherishes so much— reading those truths from my soul.

Finally, perhaps because I knew I would not have to face her for a while, I was able to tell her what she has meant to me, what she will continue to mean to me. And I didn't even stop to think about her rules for writing! Once I started, I couldn't stop…

And now I am on my way to the airport for my last glimpse of her before she leaves. The weather has cleared, but the skies are still threatening as I wheel my truck into a parking space. And I am early. Almost always when we met, she was there first, so it is some kind of irony that she will notice—my being there, waiting for her.

I am standing across from her departure gate, leaning against the wall in the main corridor, holding that single rose. People surround me, but I am alone with my thoughts.

They say, here in America, that what goes around comes around. That phrase echoes in my mind when I see her. She has on the same blue suit she wore when I first saw her, and she is walking with those same confident strides I love to watch. There is a man on either side of her; and I don't know which is Wil and which is Simon, but I know that's who they are. One of them carries her black mink coat, folded over his arm; and the other, her carry-on case. She is laughing and talking with them both; buoyant, I think, is the word. A word from the sea again. I watch her approaching through that interminable airport corridor for a long time before she sees me.

I am remembering moments from our times together, feeling the joy she always brings me, and I want to run away, not have her see me, see what I think must be showing on my face—which she can read so well. But I stay. It is my parting gift—to let her know finally and surely that I love her as she is leaving.

I am remembering that night at the concert when I stood against another wall and watched this elegant woman who gives so much of herself to me. I remember the glory of that night—the music in the concert hall, our own music which we created together after the concert, and I know no one will ever touch me in quite the same way. The vision of her standing against the windows of the glass dome passes before me, and the images of that weekend are a movie playing on a screen only I see.

I know I love this woman who passes me as if she does not know me, with a man on each side of her. Only her eyes meet mine, and I know she is feeling me inside her as she misses a step; she is inhaling me, as I am smelling her from thirty feet away, tasting my lifeblood as my tongue moves in my own mouth at the thought of her. Her carriage is erect. She is proud. She belongs to me as she has never belonged to another. Yet she passes by, and only she and I know that her panties—those wonderful silk panties—are damp and sticky with desire for me, and I long so much for her that I find I am pressing myself against this wall to keep from running after her. So much for her freedom and mine...

The passengers line up to board; hugs and kisses then for the men who have come to see her off. Just as she passes through the door and almost out of sight, she turns and blows a kiss as if to the world in general, but that one is mine. The two men walk back the way they have come, past me once again but without their treasure—two more anonymous men in this airport who are totally unaware of this invisible me—another anonymous man.

I wait until the boarding is done, and then approach the boarding agent at the door. Would she please give this rose to Justina Packard, the woman in the blue suit in first-class? She hesitates, then says, "Oh, why don't you go do it yourself? We're going to be late taking off, but hurry back out anyway."

So I see her, her eyes full of unshed tears now that she is alone, her head resting on the seat, staring. I wonder what it is she sees and gently kiss that mouth as I lay the rose in her lap. The tears cascade gently down her cheeks as she greedily kisses me in return. "Sweet one, I can't stay. I promised I'd only be a minute. I love you." And I am gone.

Outside, I see the storm has returned, and it is the kind of downpour that creates instant flooding. I turn on the radio for news of street closures, then turn it off. I am content with the silence. If I stay on the freeways, I think I'll manage. I should be home within the hour. With my new job and my irregular hours, Anna is not so likely to question where I've been, and with this storm, she will also expect me to be late. How much I've changed, precipitated change in my own household, and how much of that is adjustment to my new job, I can't guess. But my life at home seems to be improving, even if it's not loving. Justina deserves some credit for this, reminding me constantly to be open and accepting of the kids and of Anna herself.

Justina, sitting in her seat, staring with eyes full of tears, my rose on her quiet lap, flashes alternately on my windshield between the sweeps of the wipers. I see us reflected in each other's eyes as we have so often been, and I see also that every love is first love, a new love, shaping our lives and our futures. Whether we rush headlong to embrace it as Justina does or resist it as I do, we are captive and forever changed. As always, when I leave Justina and turn homeward, I am humming... She had to go, but she is not gone from me forever, and she now knows I love her.

And even tonight, especially tonight, I wonder what the lake is like with the wind blowing and the rain slashing at its waters, but I dutifully turn into my driveway. I switch off the engine and sit in this one silent place which is all my own, letting the evening's events wash over me, much as the rain washes over my truck. When the rain finally quits, my truck will bear the effects of this downpour—mud and white irregular circles—mineral deposits or toxic rain—spots all over—I don't care. I am cleansed—innocent and untarnished—loving Justina. And I contemplate the irony and incongruity of our love—illicit—sinful as Justina would quickly remind me—that is so pure that it has the power to visit me with this metamorphosis.

CHAPTER FIFTEEN

I am late to work the next morning. I stopped to have the truck washed of the ravages of the storm to match that purity I am feeling this morning. I do not even turn on the radio. I want no voices, no sounds, for these few minutes before work when I can revel in this joy I feel.

When I arrive, a florist has already been there before me to deliver a single red rose with a poem—from Justina, of course—in Greek:

Τό χαμόγελο
Καταφαγωμένο, αποκωμένο, σβησμένο, ξεφρουδιομένο από
τά κύματα...
Λάμψη, Σύγκρουση, Πιτσίλισμα και συντριβή στη θάλασσα
μέ τά δακρυά μου...
Ελαφρό, λυπημένο, φιδίσιο άλας στό μάγουλό μου
η αλμύρα...
Από τήν απέραντη θάλασσα της αγάπης μου γιά σένα
καρδιά...
Εύθραυστη, αδύνατη, αγωνιούσα, τρελή, έξαλλη
χωρίς εσένα...

And while I sit there at my desk, pondering, once again, how she does these things, I can feel those tears, wanting to be released, yet unshed, but they are so sweet and not sorrowful. I've taken some kidding from my colleagues about the delivery of the rose, and though ordinarily it would have annoyed me, it seems nothing can destroy the good feeling that engulfs me. So I carry on with them, making small jokes about who sent it and embellishing the stories with exaggerated claims about unknown admirers, pretending there are so many of them I wouldn't know which one could have sent it.

Amidst the buffoonery, Michael wheels into the doorway, waiting, with a look on his face that is frightening. I wonder immediately if he has had bad news. Has he been dismissed? I can't imagine what is causing that look, and the jokers around me are reluctant to leave before they get in another jab at my supposed secret life, but finally, they are all gone.

Michael closes the door after he wheels himself inside and looks at me silently, painfully for a moment, then says, "Sasha, you haven't heard..."

"Heard? Heard what? What's happened?"

"Do you know about the plane that crashed last night? There are no survivors..." I did not really hear his next words... "Justina is listed among the passengers."

EPILOGUE

EPILOGUE

Justina has been dead for a month. A long, horrible month in which I can find no consolation. How can I grieve for someone who never existed so far as anyone knows? To whom can I turn for help? And I know I don't want help from anyone. I want to be alone, and once again I think of that warm cylinder of water where I can go and forget. I try pretending she is only in New York—that I wouldn't have that much contact with her even if she were alive, but my heart and soul are not so easily deceived.

Michael knows, but since he was the messenger of the devastating news, he is also pained remembering my shock and my reaction—covering for me, pretending I was ill and getting me out of the plant. I don't remember who he talked to, what he told them. I have a vague recollection of Carol appearing in my office and leading me out to Michael's car. Isn't it ironic? Michael, in his wheelchair, taking care of his now disabled friend.

When he asked what he could do for me, I asked him to take me to a motel—Justina's and my place—and he was kind enough to leave me when I asked him to. We never talked about it again, and now he's too concerned about me to speak—and I can't. I know he feels for me, but I can't handle his grief for me as well as my own. I have returned to closing myself up once again.

As I lay on that bed in the motel alone where Justina and I loved each other—the sheet pulled over my head, the drapes drawn, my eyes closed, in whatever darkness I could make, I am frozen—feeling the absence of feeling. In those early hours, I descended into a black hole where I was content to stay forever. But that wasn't even a conscious thought. I was bereft—immobile—empty...

And then—I don't know how much later—I felt the bottoms of Justina's toes gently caressing the tops of my feet, as she was wont to do when we were lying together, haunting me—haunting, yet comforting. I could smell her as surely as if she were there alongside me. I was afraid to move—to have her disappear from me...

Finally, I cried into this phantom of her...

In my mind's eye, I saw my roses all over her apartment, now a funeral offering instead of the gift I meant it to be at the altar of our love. And I can't wash away the guilt of not letting her know how I felt sooner—but I wasn't ready to admit it to myself—for waiting to send her a letter she would never read. Too late, Sasha, too late...

If I was weary before, I have now added depression and this consummate grief to the weariness. Some part of me, the best part of me is dead, but I go on living. It is as I always feared. If I learned to live in the joy of life and exult as Justina did, I would forever be plagued by the demons around me and be worse off when it was taken away—as I forecast it would be. What is it she was always saying? "To know—to know everything, Sasha!" Now I know what it can be like, but will not be. Such knowledge is my curse!

It is late morning and I am sitting in my office, staring into space, when the phone rings. It is the receptionist telling me Natalie Packard has arrived for her appointment. At the sound of that name, my eyes seek the single dead rose in the florist's vase on my book case. I swallow hard, and I feel, as I do so often lately, unable to stand, to function. But my body obeys; I rise and go out to the lobby.

Natalie is a worse shock—with all the facial and body characteristics of her mother. It is as if a young Justina has returned from the grave. I remember where I am and motion her to come with me after our greeting. I don't know why she is here, how she knows who I am, how she came to find me, so I am distressed on that count as well.

I close the door behind us and pull out a chair for her. "How can I help you?"

"Oh, not at all," she replies. "I have a letter for you—at least I suppose it's a letter—from my," and she pauses painfully before she can go on, "late mother. I don't know if you are aware that she was killed in a plane crash about a month ago, and I don't know who you are, but when we went through her safety deposit box, there were letters in there for each of us—personal messages should she die before us."

I could feel my grief, bitter and sour in my throat, twisting at my soul, threatening to be made public, but by now I was getting used to swallowing hard, not giving it the display it desired.

She gathered her courage, sighed deeply, as I had known Justina to do, then continued. "Mine was by far the largest of the batch because it contained my letter and this one for you. She asked me to hand deliver it to you at work if that was at all possible, and if it was not, I was to burn it without reading it." And she passed a letter-sized envelope with my name on it written in Justina's hand. I recognized her stationery. I could not bear to touch it with her daughter sitting before me, so I left it where it lay.

"And Simon Aldridge—do you know who he is?—gave me this envelope to deliver to you at the same time." And she handed me a larger manila envelope which was sealed, about the size of my passionate purple envelope to Justina. I knew at a glance it was the letter I'd sent ahead to New York being returned.

She waited. Did she want me to open them? I took the second envelope and laid it alongside the other on my desk in front of me and thanked her. I was numb. What did she know?

She was having trouble composing herself. "How are you doing?" I asked gently.

"Not very well. She was the most important person in my life and I keep wondering how I will manage without her."

"Yes, I know," I said quietly.

She looked up, eyebrows raised. "You know she was the most important person in my life? Or what?"

"Yes, I knew that. In many ways you were that important to her, too." I avoided her other question; my question also. How would I manage without her?

"How do you know that much about my mother?" The question was not impertinent, merely curious. "Were you involved with her and Simon on this project? I don't remember seeing you at the memorial service…"

And I thought, "No, because I slipped in at the back after the service started and left just as it was ending." But I said, "No, I don't even know Simon Aldridge."

"How long did you know my mother?" she asked suddenly, and I could see Justina when an unexpected thought occurred to her.

"For about a year—I was a student in one of her classes."

She looked at me quizzically, disbelieving. "And you were important enough for her to leave you a letter?"

I was trying to find an appropriate answer, trying not to look at those Justina eyes, and I began moving papers on my desk, still not touching the precious envelopes.

"No!" she said suddenly, almost violently. "You were her lover. I knew, I just knew there was someone last year when I came home for Christmas. She had lost those few extra pounds and was beautiful—suddenly giggly and gay—happy in a different way. I never said anything to her—what can you say to your mom—'Are you having an affair?'—I don't think so. But I was pretty sure that was what was going on." I remained silent. What could I say?

And then she surprised me. "Oh, thank you. She's been such fun this past year. Whenever I came home, we had such good times." She paused, remembering; then quickly, "Not that we didn't before; she was just different, more available and more mysterious at the same time. She was so happy…" She started to weep, found a tissue in her purse, and I knew I couldn't touch her, put an arm around her to comfort her. If I had, I would have cried with her to release the huge, silent, racking sobs that consumed me.

"I'm sorry for you then," she said, trying to control herself. "If you had that much of an effect on her, you must be pretty devastated yourself."

And she smiled through her tears, remembering some fun they had had together. "She could seem so ditzy at times, but she was the most passionate and intense person I'll every know. If she loved you,

you were lucky. I know she felt lucky—she said it often during that time—how lucky she was—how the gods had favored her.

"I'm glad I found you so you can have her letter. It's helped all of us. Somehow it was like her—to make sure all those she loved would have one last gift even from her grave…" She dwindled off, hesitated, began twisting the tissue in her hands.

When she realized what she was doing, she stopped, and looked up shyly. "Her ashes were sprinkled over that funny sacred mountaintop on the Indian reservation. Simon got special permission from the tribe, but she had worked there for a few years and they remembered her, so it was done." And she paused again. "Just in case you want to know where she is."

And still she sat, thoughtfully inspecting me for a few moments as if she could fathom what it was Justina saw in me, much as I had so often wondered myself. Her eyes rested on the dead rose on my bookcase, then opened wider with understanding.

"I see so much now. I was the one who went to New York with Simon to empty her new apartment. My dad just couldn't go. There were dead roses all over the place in huge vases. Roses filled her bathtub—her kitchen sink—all over her pillows and the bed. They were everywhere. I've never seen so many colors of roses, but these were newly dead if you know what I mean. The apartment manager said they were delivered the day she was to arrive— to welcome her, he supposed. And in her office, the designer who put her apartment together, said she wanted this vase of old dead roses on her desk, three red ones. They were yours, weren't they? All of them, including those three? We used to tease her about those three when she was still at home. She threatened all of us, said if anyone ever touched them they would know her wrath, and they were important enough for her to have packed and sent on ahead so they would be there…"

Her voice trailed off. "I brought them back and laid them on the sacred mountain when we sprinkled her ashes." She was quiet a few more minutes, a comfortable silence as we each sat remembering…

"I see that now that Simon tried to prepare me for you. He told me about a conversation he once had with my mom—something about the ability to love more than one person at a time—that she said something about the human capacity to love all your children, two parents, many friends, but you could only have one lover—something she didn't quite understand since she believed the more you loved, the more love you had to give…" Again she hesitated. "My mother didn't love casually, so you must be someone very special…"

Somewhere deep inside I hoped she recognized that my silence was born of my grief—my muteness, testimony to the fact that there were no words in my head—only this ineradicable pain in my depths which I knew would diminish in time but never leave me.

Then, "I'll leave now. Thank you for seeing me, and thank you for whatever you gave my mom. I hope she was as important to you as you obviously were to her." And she offered her hand. I swear I wanted never to let go of that hand—this link to Justina—but the most I could manage was my own thanks for delivering the letters.

I watched this younger version of Justina Lazlo Packard rise, gather herself together and glide out of my office. And I sat, holding her envelope to my cheek and remembering teasing her one day when she said she was gently rubbing some papers I sent her against her own. I cautioned her then about her obsession with me. Now I heard her voice from the envelope saying, as she soared and dipped over the mountaintop in my dream, "We are all alone; that's what freedom is."

I left my office with the two envelopes unopened and the one dead rose with her poem which came that morning after she left, and drove to the sacred mountain to meet her. She still had something to teach me, and I didn't have much time before dark, but what was new?

She always understood…

To

Liza

who would have been ecstatic to see this in print